when he reads to me

USA TODAY BESTSELLING AUTHOR

T. L. SMITH

"My book boyfriend reads the smutty scenes to me, what does your husband do?"

Warning

This book contains sexually explicit scenes and adult language and may be considered offensive to some readers. This book is intended for adults ONLY. Please store your books wisely, where they cannot be accessed by under-aged readers.

Blurb

I loved him from the beginning.
In the middle.
But maybe not at the end.
His love for me was full of possibilities, hopes, and dreams a girl like me wasn't accustomed to.
He was a nightmare that cracked and bled through my hands, and I stood there watching as it seeped into the ground.
Until *him*.
He put me back together.
Without even knowing he was doing so.

And he wasn't even my husband.

Chapter 1

Lissie

"I hate my husband."

Chapter 2

Lissie

**"I hate that I love the way he talks to me.
Especially since he isn't my husband."**

"**R**ead it to me," he says, sitting across from me.

I look up and see him watching me with those brown, almost chocolate-like eyes.

"*Now*," he demands.

He is always so demanding!

I lift the book, my gaze leaving him for just a moment before it finds its way back.

Gosh, this man.

He's covered in tattoos that skate up both arms. It's as if each drawing was imprinted on him, etched into his very soul, shaping the contours of his thoughts and emotions with every stroke. His beautiful, tan skin seems to be without imperfections apart from that one scar on his upper lip, which makes me wonder how it stays so... full?

He is wearing his usual black jeans and black boots, and his legs are crossed at the ankle.

His arms are folded tightly against his chest. "Read," he says again, although slightly less demanding this time.

I avert my gaze, not even bothering to care that he caught me looking.

He always does and never comments on it—it's strange, really.

He pays me well—to sit here and read to him, but I don't know why.

Not that I see much of the money.

My mind returns to the book, and I continue...

"Her hands slide up his shirt, skating over the ridges of his back before they slip down to his hips. She feels it as he sucks in a breath and loves the fact that she holds that power," I read from the book exactly as written, using inflection where needed and pausing for emphasis to bring the words to life.

"Continue," he says.

I look up again, and his eyes are glued to me, an intensity in his gaze that makes me pause for a second or two. Focusing back on the book, I take a deep breath before I start, *"To have a man, this powerful man who is all mine, come undone beneath my fingers is unlike anything I've ever experienced."*

I stop and peer up at him.

"What?" he asks, knowing I want to ask him a question.

"Have you ever come undone for a woman like that?"

Should I be asking this type of question? I guess if he can pay me to read this stuff, I have a right to ask. He does this thing with his tongue—it darts up and licks the scar on his lip, and I watch the action, wondering what it tastes like. Wondering how it would feel if *my* tongue touched that scar.

"No," he finally answers, grinding his jaw before he nods for me to continue.

"You're weird," I tell him.

"And *you* aren't reading," he throws back.

I give him my best eye roll, showing him how annoyed I am, before pushing my black hair behind my ear, then find where I left off and continue.

"He grunts something, but I'm so lost in touching him that I don't hear what he says..." I pause. *"But then I hear it clearly when he repeats it. 'My perfect little slut.' I freeze at his words. Did I really think he would say something sweeter to me? I am, after all,*

here for one thing—" I stop. "Time is up," I announce, closing the book.

"*Read,*" he says, his voice husky and commanding.

His demanding tone literally sends a shiver right through me.

"No." I look him directly in the eyes.

"Do you speak to *him* this way?" he asks, his head tilting to the side. His mouth is pressed into a straight line with no hint of playfulness or anything else. He doesn't really give me much of anything, never has, even though I have known him longer than my husband. "Your husband. Do you speak to him this way?"

"You know I don't," I snap as I stand. Milo has seen me with Cody more than once.

"You should take some of that fucking attitude you have for me and throw it his way." He stands, walks to the door, and holds it open. "Now, leave."

"I was going anyway." I reach for my bag, pulling the strap over my shoulder, before I walk over to him.

He's taller than me—always has been. I've known Milo for years, longer than I've known my husband. Back then, though, he was just one of those boys who was always in trouble, and I guess that hasn't really changed. He still gets into trouble, but now he's a man. And not only is he a man, he's a fucking scary one.

Terrifying.

Spine-chilling.

Deadly.

He's head of the local chapter of a motorcycle club, and even the police fear him.

"Good," he says and waits for me to walk past.

Feeling the anticipation build with each step, as I reach him, I take a deep breath. His scent envelops me, a captivating blend of rich leather and something fresh, like an ocean breeze on a summer's day. The combination is intoxicating, grounding me but also sending a thrill through my senses.

"Goodnight, Milo."

His tongue slides over his teeth as he looks down at me.

"Goodnight, Elizabeth." No one calls me Elizabeth. Only him, and no matter how often I try to correct him and tell him to call me Lissie, he never listens.

He shuts the door behind me, and the click echoes into the quiet night. I glance back as I reach my car, taking in the stillness around me. The parking lot of the clubhouse is usually bustling with club brothers, but no one is here. It's like we are wrapped in a cocoon of secrecy while I'm here, and I love that it's just us. I breathe in the cool night air as I unlock my car, and I can't help but smile, knowing these moments are our own private bubble—ours alone.

Reading to him is my favorite job.

Even if he hates me.

Even if my husband hates him.

Chapter 3

Lissie

"I just wanted him to tell me how much he loved me. The things I would do for those words..."

"**Y**ou're finished early. Luckily, he paid already," Cody, my husband, mumbles, barely glancing up at me as I walk in the door. His eyes remain fixated on the computer—porn being his go-to most nights. This man—my so-called husband—he stopped seeing me a long time ago when he realized what he could get out of me.

Or better yet, what I *let* him get out of me.

As the years go by, our marriage gets worse. Each passing day feels like another brick in the wall between us, solidifying our indifference toward each other.

I wonder why I stay.

Putting my bag on the counter, I pull open the fridge and find it empty. Nothing new there.

Turning back to Cody, who is still glued to his computer, the noises emanating from the surround-sound speakers are unmistakable, so I call his name. He doesn't listen.

"Cody, where is the food?" I ask, trying to keep the frustration out of my tone. He was supposed to go grocery shopping. He told me he would.

Cody barely looks up from the computer. A dismissive wave signals his indifference. "Fuck off, Lissie, I'm working," he says, and I watch in disgust as he reaches into his pants and pulls out his cock. His hand circles his shaft, and he starts to stroke it.

He hasn't touched me for years, not that I'm complaining. I know I'm not with him because I love him. I'm with him because he manipulated my young heart when it was at its most vulnerable, and then he put me in a position where it's hard to walk away.

Even though I know I should.

Cody is my pimp.

I think that's the best and only way to describe what he is to me now. We sleep in separate beds, bringing even more distance to a fractured marriage.

He charges for the time I spend reading with Milo. I refused to have sex with Milo, even though he's never asked. That much I stood my ground on.

I'm twenty-five and have realized I need to leave this relationship—evict myself from it. The thought has been growing in my mind, festering like rotten fruit and gaining strength with every disappointment.

Cody grunts, and I sneer at him as two women take up his screen while he strokes his cock.

Working.

Ha! Yeah, whatever.

He's probably out fucking whatever is served up to him, and I would never question it—to be honest, I don't care.

When I was seventeen, I found my mother dead in her bed, with her wrists slit and blood soaked into the sheets. She always had issues, but I never realized how bad they were.

I should have.

Cody had entered my life just before my mother took her life. He was older, charming, and knew what to say, and he was everything a young girl was looking for—trouble and fun. It didn't immediately start off hot and heavy, but soon, that's the direction it took.

Cody had a car; he had access to alcohol, drugs, and all the other things that would eventually numb my heart and mind from the pain of not knowing how to save my mother.

Or why I couldn't.

He would buy me flowers once a week, and in return, I would let him touch me. I thought I was in love with him. He thought of me when no one else cared, and that drew me to him.

It was fun, and when I turned eighteen, he asked me to marry him. I said yes immediately, and then he took all my mother's money that I received from selling her house and blew it.

And the most fucked-up part?

I let him.

Shaking my head, I grab my bag and stride to the door. The idiot doesn't even notice I'm leaving.

"You should take some of that fucking attitude you have for me and throw it his way."

Milo's words hit me with such force that I pause with my hand on the doorknob and glance back at Cody.

He comes, white semen shooting from the top of his cock—

His fucking ugly cock. The noises he makes disgust me so much that I make a gagging sound.

At the sight of my revulsion, I turn away, slamming the door as I leave. The loud bang echoes with the finality of my decision.

Fuck him.

I work for him and do what he says for the sole reason I owe him.

Nothing more.

Nothing less.

My sister needed help.

She got into deep debt and asked me for money, thinking I had some left over from the sale of our mother's house. But when she asked me, I was high. She didn't know Cody, and I wasted all the money. But Cody—slimy, disgusting, manipulative Cody— was next to me at the time and offered her money. I was too shocked at his words to tell her I didn't have it. I thought at first maybe Cody did; little did I know it was merely another trap.

Money we didn't have.

And now, to pay back the debt he owes, *I* work it off.

Little by little.

Piece by piece of my damaged soul.

I chip away at what's left of me, sacrificing my dreams and happiness for his mistakes.

My sister has no idea that we owe money to the Savage Villain's MC, which is the club where Milo is the president. She's in law enforcement, and if she found out where the money came from, not only would it affect her, it would affect us as well. I'm pretty sure she would never want to come near me again, and I don't think I could handle that. She's all I have left, one of the only people Cody hasn't destroyed my relationship with.

Cody is a pimp for other women too, but not in the same way he is for me. His other women don't read to men, they fuck them. And while he has tried to make me do the same, I've refused, much to his chagrin.

Walking down the street, I grip my bag to my side, wondering how much money I have in there. *Shit, will I be able to even afford a loaf of bread?*

I shake my head, wondering how my life is still like this.

Why do I stay? I think it's because I'm used to how my life is, and more importantly, I'm afraid of change. I'm afraid I will have no one again if I leave him or he leaves me. I never had my sister to rely on. Growing up, it was only my mother and me. My sister is ten years older than me and was raised by her father.

"Lissie." I hear my name as I reach the center of town.

I've lived in this small town all my life. It's quaint and the kind of place where everyone knows your name. The trees on Main Street are old, and their gnarled branches tell stories of decades gone by. They all have fairy lights strung through them, casting a warm, magical glow on the brick buildings with their faded signs and flower boxes behind them. The buildings are mostly historic and aren't allowed to be demolished, despite the fact that some of them should be. And while parts of it are beautiful, it also has areas that are nothing but darkness.

I lift my head to find Vogue, a friend from school, holding her round belly. She once worked for Cody, not long after we got married, but disappeared on him shortly after that. I only remember because he was complaining about it.

"It's good to see you. You look well." Her words are condescending, and rudeness is etched in her tone. I know she hates the tattoos on my skin and the way I hardly wear makeup. Despite knowing she thinks she's better than me with her piled-on makeup and designer clothes, I smile at her anyway. She was one of the cool girls in school—I most definitely was not.

Now she is married to some lawyer and clearly having his baby.

"Good to see you, too." I go to step past her, but she moves in front of me, blocking my path.

I'm trying to count how many coins I think are in the bottom of my bag when she says, "Where are you living now?"

"With my husband," I say, confused, because she knows exactly who Cody is. She tried to sleep with him just after we got married.

"Cody?" she asks, her brows rising in surprise.

The revving of bikes makes us both turn. I stare at the group of over ten Harley-Davidson bikes approaching. The townspeople are used to them, but I still look. Even after all these years, I still watch *him*. He's always at the front, always in his black leather. He gets closer, and I know from behind that helmet, he sees me as well.

"Lissie." Vogue smiles at me, but behind that smile is a flicker of something else.

I've torn my attention away but feel a distinct need to leave. Immediately. "I have to go," I say, stepping past her this time and heading straight for the local grocery store.

Walking into the store, I pass the cashier before heading past the frozen food aisle and straight to the stand that holds the bread. Searching for the cheapest loaf, I grab it and then quickly open my purse to fish out the coins I saw at the bottom. Counting them, I am short, but just barely. Dropping to my knees, I tip my bag upside down. A book falls out, and my empty and very sad purse falls with it.

Shit.

My hands are pressed to the dirty floor, and I take a deep breath to try to center myself. I put my purse back in my bag, but as I reach for the book, someone else grabs it before I can. The first thing I note are black boots, followed by a pair of black jeans I know all too well. He picks up the bread that's next to me and walks to the cashier. Still kneeling on the floor, I watch as he adds a few other items before he pays for it, and the cashier puts it all in a bag. Managing to stand on shaky legs, I walk over to him and hold out my hand.

"Do you think I got this for you?" he asks, holding the bag. He scoffs, and his voice is dripping with contempt.

Milo Savage is mean and cruel.

But there is something more behind those chocolate eyes.

"I want my book back."

He glances down at the book in his other hand, then raises his gaze back to me. "No."

He turns and strides out.

I gasp and run after him.

His crew, if that's what they're called, are all waiting for him. I feel all their eyes on me as I tap him on the shoulder. He turns to face me, and those dark, tormenting eyes lock on mine as he glares down at me. "What?" he growls out the word with a sharp edge of irritation followed by his eyes narrowing.

I hold out my hand, and a few of his men start to whistle.

Milo's gaze flicks to my hand before it comes back to mine. He bends down until he's in my face, then speaks, "No."

Sucking in a breath, I lunge for the book, but he tucks his arm behind him, putting it out of reach, but his face is still dangerously close to mine.

"Fucking with Cody's wife, are we?" One of his men laughs.

"She's married to Cody?" I hear another say, and my face flushes with embarrassment at their words. While I know some of the men, I don't know all of them. After my mother died and I married Cody, I stayed in our house for years, getting high, drinking, and not living my best life.

I've been clean for at least two years.

I touched my husband once after that and

quickly realized I hated even the thought of his touch. I was physically revolted.

Thankfully, he never forced me in that way, but he did use to force the drugs on me. And the manipulation? Yeah, he's good at that as well.

"Get angry, Elizabeth," Milo says. "Get fucking angry." He turns and throws his leg over his bike.

I have been angry for years.

Angry for the situation I'm in.

Angry, wondering when I can leave.

Angry, deciding when I should leave my deadbeat husband.

Chapter 4

Milo

"If she only knew the power she held."

My little inked-up devil.

That's how I think of her when I see her.

Why she hides herself away for that asshole and makes herself smaller when he's around, I will never know.

"Give it back, Milo. *Now*." She steps up closer to where I sit on my bike.

I shoved her book under my vest, close to my chest, for safekeeping. "Get on," I tell her, tapping the back of the bike.

"Wh-what?" she stutters.

"Get *the fuck* on." I hate to repeat myself.

She shakes her head and steps away.

"You have two choices. You either go home to

your husband…" her lip twitches at my words, "… or you get on and come with us."

Loud revving breaks through the air as the guys start their bikes.

I stare at her, waiting for her to decide.

Elizabeth Petal.

Probably the most stunning woman I will ever see in my life, yet she has no fucking clue how beautiful she is. This woman standing defiantly in front of me has long black hair that almost reaches her ass, and it falls around her heart-shaped face. And those long eyelashes flutter every time she speaks to me. Tattoos are scattered randomly up her arms. And like me, she always wears black. Tonight, she's wearing black tights, with a crop top of the same color that shows her midriff, revealing the ink on her stomach that scrolls up toward her ribs.

And don't even get me started on her lips.

Or those stormy green eyes.

When she gets mad, like she is right now, they take on a hint of gray.

"I can't," she whispers.

I lean a little closer to her. "Your husband won't care. I'll pay you for your time."

"You only pay for me to read to you. Why change it?"

"Fucking hell, Elizabeth." I shake my head, kick the bike off its stand, and start it up.

"My book," she says, barely loud enough for me to hear over the bike's engine.

"Fuck your book. It's mine now," I tell her. Then I drop the bag of food to the ground at her feet and take off. My bike is fishtailing, and my tires are squealing before I ride away.

And I leave her standing there, staring after me.

Chapter 5

Lissie

"Tell me your dark and dirty secrets, and maybe I'll share mine."

"I want a divorce," I tell Cody that night as I walk into the house, carrying the bag of groceries. I wasn't sure I was going to pick the bag up at first, but I had to because I was so fucking hungry. Cody raises his head and eyes me. His cock now back in his pants is my only reward.

"No." Just the one word before he focuses back on his damn computer screen. I hear the sounds of porn coming from the speakers like before, only this time, he turns the volume up a notch.

Cody has been my husband for a long time, and for half of those years, I may have thought I loved him.

Now, I know I never really did.

Our relationship is nothing but a series of business transactions I don't get a cent from, and I struggle to buy my own fucking food.

"Your sister called, and she's on her way over. Clean up the kitchen," he barks. I cringe as he looks up at me from his seat at the table.

Cody doesn't even glance at the bag in my hand or ask me why I have it or how I afforded it—he simply does not care.

Walking to the kitchen, I pull out the contents of the bag Milo left me and place the bread on the counter. Then I pull out the peanut butter, which he obviously bought as well. Smiling, I go to throw the bag out when I spot one piece of candy sitting at the bottom of the bag. It's the same brand of candy I've eaten numerous times at his clubhouse when I go over there to read to him.

Grinning at the single piece of white chocolate, I place it in my pants pocket and move to the toaster to toast myself some bread. My stomach is growling, and the need for food is overwhelming. I look up as Cody stands, shuts down his computer, and turns to face me. The look on his face is one of pure disdain, his eyes cold and unforgiving as he glares at me.

"I've ordered pizza," he says, watching me. "We aren't getting divorced," he adds.

"Why not?" I question. "We don't even love each other," I remind him.

"Who cares about love? You owe me, Lissie. You are *not* leaving."

"I don't owe you shit. She does," I snap.

He reaches for the closest thing to him and throws it across the room. The plate smashes against the wall, and I flinch, casting my gaze away from him.

"Would you like me to tell your sister where we got the money?"

"No." I glare at him, my eyes burning with anger and defiance.

He smirks, reveling in his power while my fists clench at my sides, every muscle taut in response to his smugness. "That's what I fucking thought. Now, act like a well-behaved woman and not a damn child," he says.

I stand there, livid, as he walks off to his room down the hall. We live in a modest two-bedroom house—it's nothing fancy, but enough for both of us. He says we don't have lots of money, but he refuses to let me get a job so I can be available for Milo when he needs me.

I've been reading to Milo for a year. It started with just your average fiction books, which lasted for a good six months, and then we dipped our toes into fantasy. But recently, we've moved on to books that are heavier on romance.

I hate it as much as I love it.

When I leave Milo, I'm usually clenching my thighs together. The way he sits there quietly and listens to me, his demeanor mostly soft and attentive, makes me feel like I am being truly heard. Most of the time, his eyes are closed, but lately, they've been open and watching me.

It's intimidating.

He is intimidating.

I know Milo from school. He's older than me, and we never had any classes together, but he was never someone to be missed. The man was popular back then, and now? Well, he basically owns this town. I don't think anyone would be stupid enough to go against him.

But my husband is pretty stupid.

A knock comes on the door, and I expect it to be the pizza, but when I open it, my sister is standing there dressed in her police uniform, smiling at me.

It's amazing to me how she changed her life around, how she went from being reliant on drugs to now being fit and clean. It gives me hope that one day soon, I will leave this god-awful place and never look back.

"Gosh, you look good," she says, reaching for me. Savannah looks so much like our mother. Her eyes are soft like Mom's were, whereas mine are sharp. Her hips are perfectly proportioned, while I barely have any shape to mine. I let her wrap me in her arms and hug her back.

Fuck, it's been so long since I've had physical contact with anyone. Cody doesn't touch me, let alone hug me. I hardly have any friends, and the only other person I speak to more than Cody is Milo, and he usually just sits there and demands words from me.

Somehow, that man demands that I speak, and when he does, it feels like my voice is actually worth listening to.

We pull apart, and I shut the door behind her as she steps inside.

"Sorry, I came straight from work," Savannah says. She moved a few towns away, and it takes her over two hours to visit, so she doesn't come often. But I know she feels obliged to since Cody helped her out all those years ago.

"How are you?" she asks, looking around for

Cody. "Happy?" Her voice is a little quieter on the last word.

"There you are, just in time. The pizza is almost here," Cody says as he appears from the hallway.

Another knock comes on the door, and Cody walks past us, pulls out cash, and hands it to the delivery guy before he takes the pizzas. "I have to head out. Work stuff," he says, placing the pizzas on the table. He comes up to me and leans in, his mouth dangerously close to mine. "Behave," he whispers.

Savannah doesn't know half of what goes on. Actually, I'm unsure if she knows anything.

Cody's lips touch my cheek instead, and he pulls back, offering a wave to Savannah, before he nods and leaves.

"Sister time," Savannah says. "This is..." she glances around, "... unusual." The smell of the food hits my stomach, and it grumbles loudly. Savannah laughs and heads straight for the pizza. "You didn't have to wait for me to eat."

I didn't, but she doesn't need to know that. Sitting opposite her, I grab a slice and take a bite, not waiting for her to grab her own.

"So I was wondering, do you have a spare change of clothes around here I could wear?" I look at her, confused. She nods to her uniform. "I want to take you out, and Cody isn't here to tell you no."

"I'm tired," I tell her around a mouthful of pizza. "I don't want to go out."

It's a lie.

I want to run.

Far, far away.

Away from the torment of my unbearable life.

But I stay where I am.

Because my asshole husband has information on her. Information that could ruin her life. Just when she's finally sorted it all out for the better.

He has videos of Savannah using drugs. He even recorded her taking the money to pay the debts back.

She is the only family I have left.

So I have to stay.

I have to protect her.

Cody wasn't always an ass, but he has his ways of keeping me tied to him. And he knows it.

What if Savannah found out?

What if I walked in to find her the same way I found our mother?

I'm not sure my heart could take that again.

I was so lost the first time that I know the second time I'd be a wreck. And a complete slave to Cody, of that I am sure. More so than I am already. *Is that possible?*

"Lissie." I peer up at her and smile. It's forced, which I'm sure she knows. "Why do you stay?"

Words are on the tip of my tongue—the words I can't tell her. "S-sorry, what?" I splutter instead. She has never asked me about my relationship. Not once. I know she knows I'm not happy here, but again, she has never asked me about it either.

"Cody, and you. Why do you stay?"

I wipe my mouth and place the rest of my slice of pizza down.

"I'm married," I remind her.

"Yes, but you aren't happy. So I ask again... why do you stay?"

"How do you know I'm not happy?" I challenge, raising a brow.

"Rumor has it that Milo has someone he pays to keep him company. I was asked if it was you."

My mouth drops open in shock, but I quickly recover. "This isn't even in your jurisdiction," I reply, my face heating up.

"Yes, but the Savage Villain's MC are known statewide."

I bite my lip and sit back.

"Why are you at Milo Savage's, Lissie? You know who he is, and how dangerous he is."

"I still live in this town, Savannah. And he may be scary to some, but not to me," I say, shaking my head. It's only a half-truth. Milo does scare me, but not in the way she might think.

She tsks. "That's probably your first mistake, thinking that man isn't dangerous."

She picks up a slice of pizza and sways it around before she says, "Stay away, please. Tell Cody to keep an eye on you, or I will."

This time, when I bite my lip, it bleeds.

Chapter 6

Milo

"I'll watch you take your last breath and smile."

"**P**rez." I look up at my prospect, Aiden, as he approaches me.

The party has started, and women are everywhere. Once a week, I let the boys loose, and we celebrate because you can't run a fucking empire without having respect from your men.

My father was the president of this MC, and when he died, I took his place. I learned everything there was from him, even if he was a fucking asshole. I have no siblings, but these men are my fucking family. They would die for me. And you can't say that's not better than some family.

The club's compound is made up of several small buildings with a larger two-story clubhouse at the center. The clubhouse contains a bar, and a pool table for the guys. It isn't the cleanest of places, but no one seems to mind. Letti, our bartender, helps keep it tidy when she's here.

A lot of the times, the club whores clean up—whoever is sober enough the next day after they crawl out of one of the guys' rooms. This place is not my full-time residence, as it is for some, but I stay here a lot. This is also where *she* comes to read to me. My room is in a building out back, behind the main garage.

"He's here," Aiden announces. *Of course, he is. That fucking slimy piece of shit.* "Let him in or kick him out?" he asks.

I give Aiden a wave, and he nods before he turns and heads to where I know that piece of shit will be located. I wait with a drink in my hand, as my men talk shit with whatever woman is their flavor tonight, for Cody to enter.

I wish I could slice his fucking throat right here right now, watch as he begs and bleeds out in front of me, and I wouldn't lift a finger to help him.

I hate him.

Not because he has *her*.

But because of who he is in general.

What she ever saw in that piece of crap, I will never know.

I watch as Aiden walks in, Cody right behind him. Cody's eyes scan the large, open room. I sit near the pool table, my hands on the bar, my head angled so I can keep him in my sights. When that sleazy gaze of his falls on me, he offers a nod in greeting, which I don't return. Why the fuck would I? *Scum.*

He walks over to my VP, Morris, and leans in. Morris, who I went to school with and is the same age as me, joined my father's MC at the same time I did. We've never been apart, and if anyone knows me best, it's Morris.

Morris's gaze flicks to me as Cody speaks, and I shake my head at him. He pulls back and says something to Cody, which deepens his frown even further. Then that piece of shit turns to me. I watch from my spot at the bar as he takes a deep breath, his Adam's apple bobbing, before he puts one foot in front of the other and walks over to me. I don't bother getting up. There is no point because we're at eye level, even with me sitting on the stool.

"I need drugs," he says, clear as day.

"We have supplied your shipment already, Cody." I tap the wooden bar as Letti, who is Morris's sister, starts making me a drink.

"Come on, man, please," he begs. "I'll send Lissie over now. Will that help?" I grimace at his words, reminding myself not to kill him. While he may be useful, he is a fucking idiot. Cody is our biggest drug dealer, a fact that I'm not even sure Lissie knows. Last week, he got a shipment, and he's already here asking for more. I haven't gotten payment for the last supply, so there is little chance of that.

"You expect me to take your wife as a form of payment?" I ask, shaking my head.

"You have before."

Letti slides my drink toward me, and I look at the heavy glass and think about smashing his head in with it. "Payment first, then we talk product," I tell him.

"I don't have it. The girls are late. But I have more clients," he insists before scratching his chin. To me, it looks like he's using more of the product than he's selling. I clench my jaw as Morris walks over.

"You need to leave *now*! And don't come back unless you have payment," Morris says, tapping Cody on the shoulder.

"Please. She can come immediately," he relays.

"*Now*," Morris growls.

"Fucking hell! Just take the bitch as payment," Cody shouts.

That's all it takes for me to lift the glass, still full

of my favorite whiskey, and smash it straight into his fucking nose. Everything quiets down around us as a scream rips through him, and his hands go up to protect his face from me damaging it even more. His bloodshot eyes glare at me, and I see the anger but more so the fear there.

"Don't come back until you have payment. Or next time, I will break both your fucking legs and your nose again for good measure." I sit back down and tap the bar. Letti pours me another drink as Aiden escorts Cody, the slimy fuck, out of my clubhouse.

Chapter 7

Lissie

"Sometimes love is just a lie."

"**G**et the fuck out of bed."

The snarling tone pulls me from my sleep. My hands clutch the blanket tightly when he repeats them, but this time with more venom and intensity. The room feels colder, and a shiver runs down my spine as his disgusting vileness fills the air. My heart races, and I brace myself for what's coming.

Cody hasn't hit me before, but he has pushed me. The one thing that works best on me, which he knows, is when he degrades me. When he tells me how the only person I have is him and he's amazed that my sister hasn't killed herself yet.

When he says those words...

Well, that's part of what makes me stay.

Who would I have?

Could I live with having no one?

But then there is that small part of me who knows I would be fine if I left him. My sister may hate me at first, and her life might crumble, but she would be alive.

"*Now*, Lissie. Get the fuck up," he yells once more. The blanket is torn from my grip and thrown to the floor. I hear his heavy footsteps as he goes to turn on my bedroom light. Sitting up in bed, the cold seeps into my bare legs while I look at him. He has dried blood all over his face, and his nose is bent at a weird angle. A bottle of vodka dangles from one hand, and I know whatever takes place next is not going to be good for me.

"What happened?"

"*You* fucking happened. Get out of bed, *now*."

"No," I whisper.

Then I hear giggling from the living room and know he brought them home with him—the women. It's been two days since I last saw him and a week since my sister was here. Things have been quiet as usual between us, and to be honest, I didn't even bother calling or asking him where he was. I like the quiet. And now he comes into my room and demands I get up.

He sucks in air between his teeth and makes a hissing sound. "*Now*, Lissie. Get. The. Fuck. Out. Of. Bed." The words are abrupt and disconnected, and I know he's been on a bender by its sounds.

"What happened to your face?" I remain in bed and glance at the clock on my wall.

It's late—midnight. I went to sleep early tonight.

"*You* happened. I'm so fucking over you and everything you cost me." He wipes the back of his hand over his mouth before he lifts the bottle and takes a drink.

"Okay, divorce me, then."

"Oh, you'd like that, wouldn't you?" The sarcasm drips from his words, his tone laced with contempt for me. His eyes narrow—hostility radiating from him. I shrink back, biting the edge of my mouth. "So you can, what? You have never held a job, Lissie. What the fuck would you do without me?"

When I was growing up, I wanted to be an author, which I now find hilarious, considering I read to someone for money.

There is so much on the tip of my tongue that I want to tell him, so many things I have planned, none of which involve his fucking ass.

"See! *Nothing*. I feed you and clothe you. Fuck, I even give you money for those awful tattoos on your body." He shakes his head. "Get out of bed. We have work to do," he spits.

"Work?"

"Yes, you're coming with me to the clubhouse."

"It's not my night," I remind him.

"Well, now it is." He storms out, and one of his girls stops in the bedroom doorway. She peers in and looks around the room, then raises her brows at me before she turns and walks off. *Skank.*

Getting up, I shut the door, change into a pair of jeans, and throw on a sweater, not bothering to put something on underneath it. Pulling my hair into a top bun, I walk out to find two of his girls hanging off him.

All heads turn to me, and I stand silently, staring back at them. They can fuck him for all I care. Believe me, I lost interest in *that man* a long time ago. They can have at it.

He pushes them off him and stalks over to me. He reaches for my sweater and tugs on it, clearly not impressed with what I am wearing. I'm comfortable. That's all I aim for these days. I have no reason to dress up for anyone.

"Change," he orders, his red-tinged blue eyes lock on me.

"No."

His head tilts to the side. "Maybe I need to start training you better. A little fucking smack here and there should teach you."

I don't respond.

If he lays a hand on me, I'll leave. Of that, I have no doubt.

Why would it take that to make me leave? Things are bad enough as they are.

Why haven't I already left? Because I can survive with how things are. I can keep my sister sane and not let her spiral back to where she used to be by sacrificing myself. Everything I do, I do with my sister in mind.

"What he even sees in you is beyond me," he sneers, then drops his hand from my sweater and heads toward the door. The three women he came with file out after him. The door hangs open, and I follow to find them already in the car. Cody always drinks and drives, and as much as I hate it, he clearly never listens to me when I tell him not to. One day, he will get himself killed, and I hope when he does, he doesn't take any innocent people with him.

I climb into the back seat and stare out the window as the women play with the music. When they land on a song they like, they start to sing, and the one next to me bumps shoulders with me to get me to sing along. I ignore her, as I do with every woman he brings around, and continue staring out the window at the nothingness beyond.

One might wonder why I don't take the front seat, considering I'm his wife. But I am only his wife in name, not anything else. But even that part, I hate.

The car slows down, and I recognize the compound. It's currently lit up, and there are bikes and people everywhere, unlike when I am usually here.

The women spill out of the car when Cody parks. The asshole takes another swig of his alcohol and then climbs out too. I contemplate taking the keys and driving off—I'm not even sure he would realize if I did. Cody's arms are around two of the women as he sidles up closer to the men who are sitting around the fire like he's already forgotten about me.

Getting out of the car, I look down at the dead grass beneath my old sneakers and sigh.

I'd rather be in bed.

I don't even know why I'm here.

As I scan the area in front of the clubhouse, it appears no one even notices me.

I know a few of the men here from school and growing up, but not on any truly personal level. I used to be shy and nervous coming here, but now I know most of the guys, as I always pass them when I come in. Even though some don't speak to me, they all seem to be respectful, for the most part.

I walk into the clubhouse and take a seat at the makeshift bar, then reach over to grab a soda, bypassing Letti and the club members tending the bar with her. Letti is my age, though I have never really spoken to her much when we were growing up.

The guys helping her are called prospects, and basically, they do whatever the other members say and then some. They all seem happy to be here. One of them, Mason, even went to a boys' private school around here. I think he's two years older than me. I'm not sure why he joined, but I have heard stories his family owed money and were killed, and that's why. But it's all stories. I've learned not to listen to rumors, considering how many are out there about me.

"Not drinking tonight?" Mason asks.

"Are you?" I ask him, nodding to his open beer can.

"Want one?"

I'm about to say no, but I shrug my shoulders instead. "Sure."

He hands me one and smiles. Mason has a nice

smile. He still has that vibe about him that he came from money, but I know he no longer lives that lifestyle. Actually, I'm pretty sure he lives here like a few of the others. I tap on the lid of the can and take in the bar. The thick, varnished wood is polished to a sheen that I can almost see my face in it. Mason gives me a knowing look and nods to the can. I crack it open and shoot him a smile.

Just as I put the can to my lips, it's snatched from my hand. My head whips around, and I find Milo standing there with a woman attached to his side.

"Give it back," I demand, and he just looks at me. "Give it back, Milo."

He turns to Mason. "Don't give her another, do you understand?"

"Yes," Mason replies without hesitation.

"I'm allowed to drink, you asshole." I hop off the barstool and reach for it, trying to snatch it from his hand, but he holds it up in the air so I can't reach it.

"Not here, you aren't."

I contemplate punching him, but I realize that wouldn't be fair. After all, it's not him I'm angry at.

"Drink." Milo taps the bar, and Mason serves him while I watch him and smirk.

"Okay, how about a game? Every answer you get wrong, you drink. I'll do the same," I offer.

Milo side-eyes Mason as he mutters to me, "I'm not participating in getting you smashed."

"You are. If I have to be here, you and me and..." I look over his shoulder to the woman, "... whoever that is, are going to drink while my husband does fuck knows what, with fuck knows who."

"He left," Milo informs me.

I freeze because, of course, he left. He is the worst husband ever. Most husbands would hate to leave their wife at a clubhouse with only men around them.

Mine, fucking leaves.

"Go away, Cassandra," he says, and the woman seethes at him.

"That's not nice," I say to him.

"Neither is trying to watch you drown out your life with alcohol," he replies.

I give him my best eye roll. "You've seen me drunk once. I bet I'm the best drunk you ever did see. Funny, I'm sure," I remind him.

Mason chuckles. I beam at him, and he shakes his head, still laughing.

"Milo is a—" Mason starts.

"Shut it, Mason," Milo growls, cutting Mason off. Mason holds up his hands and puts up a bottle of tequila.

"Let's do a quiz," I say, smiling. "I'll go first. Every wrong answer is a shot."

"Go ahead." Milo waves his hand at me as Mason puts two shot glasses down. I smile, knowing I got him to play when he initially did not want to. He pours tequila into each and steps back.

"What's the smallest state in the USA?" I ask.

He smirks and answers, "Rhode Island."

I nod at his correct answer. We may not live there, but it's a place I have always wanted to visit.

"What country is Samsung based in?" he asks.

"South Korea," I reply with a grin. "What country's national animal is the rooster?"

He sits back and stares at the shot glasses before he lifts his gaze back to me and says, "France."

Mason whistles from behind the bar. I look at him, confused, then back at Milo.

"How many elements are there in the periodic table?" Milo questions.

"I'm changing the rules," I cut in.

"Answer..."

"Every answer I get right, you do a shot," I throw out.

"Answer..."

"One hundred and eighteen," I say, then nod to

the shot. He lifts it and drinks while Mason shakes his head, laughing.

"What is the rarest blood type in humans?" I ask.

"You couldn't have gone with something more difficult?" He raises a brow, and his tongue darts out and licks his scar. He does that a lot. "Rhnull."

I pick up the shot and drink it.

We do this until I'm on my fifth shot, and then he stops. A few people called his name during that time, but he ignored them throughout our game. It isn't until he slides water in front of me that I give him an assessing look.

"You're smart," I say.

"You're just working that out?" he asks with a raised brow. "And here I thought you were as well. Seems I was wrong."

"He's a bloody genius, is what he is," Mason butts in, coming back with more alcohol in his hands. "But you, Lissie, are just as smart."

I'm not. I ended up getting two wrong, while he never got any wrong.

"Why are you here?" I ask Milo.

Mason whistles as he walks off.

"What is that supposed to mean?" He leans in.

My vision is a little blurry as I nestle the beer in my hand. I picked up the fresh drink without him noticing. "Why aren't you off with your women?"

"Like your husband is?" he grits through clenched teeth.

"Yes, like Cody."

"Because not all of us get everything handed to us on a platter, pretty girl," he says before standing and striding off.

I sit there and drink the rest of my beer, thinking about our exchange, and I stay there for a good hour before I decide to slip away to the car. I need to sleep, and walking home is not a smart idea.

Trying to get the keys from my pocket, I remember Cody drove. My phone slips from my pocket and falls to the floor in the process. Bending down, I reach for it and hear moaning sounds. Crawling forward on my hands and knees, I see two sets of feet on the other side of the car. Moving around to the front, I stay low and quiet until I reach the other side. When I get there, I see a woman on her knees in front of a man, her head bobbing up and down. Milo has a hand gripped in her hair while his other slides through his own hair as she sucks.

It startles me when that look in his eyes meets mine. It's not like any look I'm used to.

Want and need mixing into one.

And it's dangerous to get caught up in a look like that. I back up and fall on my ass. The woman stops for a second before Milo yanks her hair, making her move again. I hurry away toward the fire pit and fall asleep to the memory of the sound he made and the look in his eyes.

When I wake up, I'm lying in a bed—one that isn't mine—and my head hurts. As I get up, I find Milo sleeping on the floor. I stumble, trying to avoid stepping on him and bang my knee against the bed. "Ouch."

"Go back to sleep," he mumbles.

"Why am I here? And where is here?" I ask, scanning my surroundings. The bed I was sleeping on was covered with white sheets and was so comfy. It's like sleeping on a cloud. And why is it so clean?

"Oh God, will you shut it? My head hurts, and the floor is uncomfortable."

"That sounds like a *you* problem," I snark, reaching for the bed again and getting back in, pulling the sheet up to hold off the morning chill that hits my skin.

He grumbles something I don't understand before he gets up, brings a pillow with him, and climbs in next to me. His stomach hits the bed, and his face smushes into the pillow.

"Fuck yes."

"No," I say, trying to push him. He needs to move, preferably out of bed. "I don't want to share a bed with you."

"Well, Pretty Lady, you either go back to sleep or try waking your deadbeat of a husband. And we both know he isn't going to come get you anyway. You and I both had way too much to drink to drive."

What time did I fall asleep?

Was the sun starting to rise when I passed out?

Gosh, my memory is bad.

"You've been asleep for two hours, and you will still have alcohol in your system, so go back to sleep and get rid of it," Milo mumbles. I notice he's wearing a white shirt and still has his black jeans on, but his vest has been discarded neatly on a cupboard.

"Stay on your side of the bed." I reach for a pillow and put it between us, not caring if it's his room or not. He doesn't reply as I lie back down next to him. It isn't long before I pass back out, with the smell of rich leather and ocean breeze surrounding me.

I'm hot. I'm pretty sure that's what wakes me. At least, that's what I'm telling myself. It's definitely not the fact that I can feel him everywhere, and I'm too afraid to open my eyes to see the position we're in.

I'm a married woman in bed with another man.

Not that it matters considering my husband is off with some other woman, nor the fact that I despise him, but still!

"You're hot." His voice echoes through me.

Snapping my eyes open, I try to move, but a pair of hands grab my hips, stopping me.

"I suggest you don't wiggle." It's then I feel his hardness pressing against me. Lifting my head from his chest, I note a wet spot on his shirt. "You drool when you sleep." I open my mouth to reply, and he shakes his head. "And your breath stinks."

"Why did you move me?" I accuse, looking into his chocolate eyes.

One dark brow raises. "Me? No, Pretty Lady, you moved, I stayed still."

"You went to sleep on your stomach," I remind him, and he shakes his head.

"No, I did not. As soon as you started snoring, I turned over and fell asleep on my back. That was until your cute ass decided the best pillow on my bed was me." When he says it, his brow rises as if to say, *I dare you to argue with me.*

"I wouldn't have." I know I move a lot in my sleep because my pillows and blankets are usually everywhere when I wake—but sleeping on him?

"Oh, you did. Next time, I'll record it for proof."

"There won't be a next time."

"So why are you still on me?" Milo licks his lips. I lift myself off him and almost fall off the bed, but he catches me, and my feet manage to land on the floor. "You can sleep on me anytime. You, my Pretty Lady, are comfy as all hell."

He stretches, and his shirt lifts, baring a strip of his abdomen. It's tanned, and he has lines indented on his lower stomach, showcasing a defined V.

"If you keep looking at me like that, I may eat you." I step back and go straight to the door. "I'll be here anytime you want me, Pretty Lady." He flops back down and falls straight back to sleep before I can reach the door.

It's quiet when I step out of his room, and I wonder how the fuck I'm going to get home.

Chapter 8

Milo

**"To see such a beauty sleep, then turn into
a gremlin... well, it's a beautiful thing."**

She watches as my tongue darts out and licks my scar, her eyes tracking every movement.

"Mr. Savage, you know you can't keep this up."

"Do I not pay enough to get me out of these things?" I remind her. Rebecca Dark has been my family's lawyer for over fifteen years. Usually, I don't have to pay a visit to her office, but today it was necessary.

"You do, sir, but when you leave witnesses who can identify you, it makes my job a lot harder."

"Who is the witness?" I ask.

She narrows her eyes at me. "You *aren't* going to kill them, Milo."

I smile at her. "Do you think you can tell me what to do, Rebecca?"

She shuffles some of her papers around and shakes her head. "I was doing no such thing. Let me handle it, and we can go from there."

I stand from the seat on the other side of her desk. "No, I think it's time I took matters into my own hands." I give her a curt nod before spinning on my heels and walking away.

She calls my name as I walk out of her office, and when I don't turn around, I hear her cuss at me, and I shake my head at the old bat. My father hired her when he was president of the MC, and while Rebecca is good, she has been lacking tremendously compared to how she was with my father.

As I walk closer, I see Morris already outside on his bike, waiting for me. He sits there, helmet in hand, watching me.

"Where are we going?" he asks with a slow and steady smile.

"To find a witness."

He nods, accepting the plan without a single question.

Two towns over, I find the man who decided it was the best decision to tell the police what he saw when he was in *my* town. I'm guessing this is his idea of hiding, and to be honest, it's the worst attempt I have ever had to unravel.

"Is he really..." Morris trails off, not sure what else to say while staring intently.

"He is." I nod.

This guy—the one who witnessed me kill someone—is standing on his front porch, music blaring, a bottle of beer in one hand and a joint in the other while he dances, naked.

It's dark as we walk down the street toward the idiot's house. We left our bikes parked two blocks away so he didn't notice us as we stepped up onto his porch. Morris takes a seat on one of the swings, and I stand at the top of the steps, blocking any escape. Usually, I would send my men to deal with any dirty work, but I have some aggression that needs to be worked out... on his fucking face.

And I am furious!

The guy takes another puff of his joint and turns his naked ass around, swinging his fucking limp cock in the air.

Luckily for him, his neighbors aren't close enough to hear whatever shit he has going on. The minute his groggy eyes open, he spots Morris, and he goes to step away but realizes I'm blocking his path.

"Hello, Huston," I say, smiling at him. His eyes go wide, and he drops the bottle of beer at his feet, trying to back up the other way. I pull the gun from my pants and point it at him.

"I wouldn't do that if I were you. I'd hate to mess up..." I wave the gun around and then point it at his cock, "... that thing."

His hands shoot down to cover his cock, but he forgets the joint in his hand, which proceeds to burn his pubic hair, giving off the most disgusting smell.

Morris stands, steps over the broken bottle and motions for Huston to go inside. He stays where he is, covering his junk as I wave the gun at him to follow Morris. He turns, his hands not moving, and steps inside past Morris. I follow and shut the door behind me.

"I know who you both are," Huston says.

"Good, we would hope for nothing less," Morris replies with a smile as he scans the room. I stand where I am at the door and watch.

"You can't kill me. They'll know it's you."

"Will they?"

His bloodshot eyes find mine. "They will. I've already given my statement." His voice is laced with panic, and his shaking hands give away how he's feeling at this moment.

"Do they still take a dead man's statement into consideration?" I ask Morris, to which he shrugs.

"Who cares."

"Yeah, who cares," I say, agreeing with him, and lift the gun and shoot Huston directly between the eyes. My father started teaching me to shoot when I was five, and now I never miss.

"Burn it down?" Morris asks.

I nod. There is nothing more to do here.

Morris walks out to our bikes and starts siphoning some gas and then walks back in the garage and splashes its contents around the living room and Huston's body before we step out, toss a lit match to the floor, and let the house burn from the inside out.

Chapter 9

Lissie

"I read for him, not to him."

Cody left—not me, unfortunately.

I ended up walking home that day when I woke in Milo's bed because Cody refused to pick me up. I knew if I asked Milo, he would take me, but I refuse to ask another man for help.

Cody left twenty dollars on the counter, which usually means I won't see him for a week. I usually love it when he goes away for his so-called 'work trips,' as he likes to call them because I get the house to myself. But the small amount of money he leaves doesn't last long, and by the third day, the bread I bought the day he left is almost gone.

Right now, my head is pounding. I haven't been

able to leave the couch for the last day, and I was due to read to Milo last night.

I did not show up.

So when I hear a knock at my door, I think it's someone for Cody, but when the knocking doesn't stop after a few minutes, the door is kicked in. I'm lying on the couch, the pain way too intense to move to see who it is. I'm sure the death they offer me will be more acceptable than the one my body is currently trying to inflict on me. I close my eyes as I hear footsteps approaching.

"You missed our appointment."

I open my eyes to find Milo staring down at me, dressed in his leather vest, his dark hair perfectly styled, and his lips pursed. "Do you not know how to answer me?" he asks.

I roll over, my body aching as I do so, and give him my back.

I feel his hand land on the back of my neck, and he mutters something I don't understand. Then I hear the door shut as he leaves, and I don't even bother wondering how the door closed if he kicked it in and how much trouble I'll be in if it is broken.

My eyes are too heavy, and they close automatically.

Darkness.

* * *

He's back.

"Take it." I look up to see Milo hovering above me, water in one hand and tablets in the other. "*Elizabeth*," he warns.

Fuck him and his *Elizabeth*.

Snatching the tablets from his hand, I swallow them without water. He shakes his head and goes to the door when someone knocks. I smell food instantly. My stomach growls, letting the world know I haven't eaten.

"Aren't you supposed to be off running motorcycles with your gang?" I ask as he returns to me. I manage to half sit up on the couch, which I haven't left for days. He pulls the side table in front of me, then swipes everything off before placing a container of Thai food on the wooden surface and it smells amazing.

"Gang?" Milo shakes his head as he grabs one of the kitchen chairs and drags it over.

"Is that what you think we are?" He opens the lid of the food container and then approaches me. Without asking, he places his hands under me and lifts me easily, then sets me back down so I'm in a sitting position. When someone else sits you up, you don't have to use as many muscles, and I hate that I appreciate him for doing that.

"I could have moved myself…" Oh God, my equilibrium is so off I have to blink my eyes before I continue, "You didn't have to touch me."

"I don't mind touching you," he replies, and I know there is another meaning behind it.

"Is that not what you are, a gang?" I ask, changing the subject.

"We don't run around the streets wearing baggy fucking clothes," he says.

I laugh, and it hurts.

I stop.

His eyes narrow at me.

"You ride around the streets wearing specific clothing, including those leather cuts you wear. So it's the same thing." I shrug. "When was the last time you fucked someone up, or worse, killed them?" I reach for the food and take a bite of the spring roll while he watches.

"Yesterday." He shows me his knuckles, which are red and angry-looking.

"And why did you do that?" He grabs a spring roll, and I stare as his lips form an O before he takes a bite.

Milo has perfect lips.

Asshole.

"He thought getting me in trouble would be a good idea." My eyes go wide at his confession.

"For what?"

"A deal gone bad" are the only words he offers.

"Is he alive?" I ask, then shake my head. "No, don't answer that."

Milo smirks and sits back. "Would you be disappointed if he was dead?"

"It's not hard to disappoint me. I do that all by myself." He stays quiet. "Do you have any kids?"

He shrugs. "Not that I'm aware of."

My mouth hangs open, and he leans over and places a finger under my chin before he lifts it up, closing it.

"I'd suggest you keep that mouth closed unless you want my tongue in it." I smack his hand away.

"How dare you." He doesn't care. He never did, so he goes back to eating.

"Where is your husband, Elizabeth?"

I shrug because I don't know.

He stands, and I can't help but notice how his black jeans move so easily with those muscular legs, and the way they fit perfectly on his hips should be illegal. I also note the absence of his leather vest. For some reason, he doesn't wear it around me. Milo steps up to the back of the couch, and that's when I see his vest. He puts it on and then comes back around in front of me.

"You tell anyone I looked after you, I'll kill them," he says, smirking.

"So you won't kill me for telling?"

His tongue darts out and touches that scar I love to watch his tongue lick. "No, just whoever knows." He winks and nods to the medicine. "Take it. If you don't, well..." He doesn't finish before he turns to leave, and I yell out after him, "Thank you, Milo."

"You could thank me with your mouth," he says, and I don't have to look at him to know he's grinning.

"No, I'm married," I reply and hear him release a breath before the door shuts.

I managed to eat some more food and then stand on shaky legs to take the leftovers to the fridge so I could eat something later since I have no money to buy anything else.

Slowly, I head back to the couch and proceed to pass out for the rest of the day.

"Fuck, everything is a mess. Have you been lying there all fucking week? And the front door? What have you fucking done? I'm going to have to fix it!" I hear Cody bark before I can comprehend what's happening.

I sit up and rub my eyes. No, *how are you? What are you doing?*

He leans down and puts his face right in mine.

"Do you remember a time when we actually liked each other?" I ask because I really want to know what he thinks. I feel like I don't even remember the last time I liked this man.

"What are you even talking about, Lissie?" He goes into the kitchen and opens the fridge, then looks back at me as I stand from the couch. "How did you afford this food?" He motions to the leftover Thai. Milo bought so much that I managed to freeze some to make it last longer.

"Do you even like me, Cody?" I question.

He shuts the fridge and goes to the front door, and I watch as he fixes the lock before he returns to me. Stopping in front of me so we are almost toe-to-toe, he leans in. "I love you."

The words taste bitter, and they didn't even leave my mouth.

"I love you, or I wouldn't support you," he says. Then he does something so unexpected I'm taken aback. His mouth moves closer, and I stand there, frozen, as it happens in slow motion. His lips land on mine, and his hand goes to the back of my head. His mouth moves against mine, and I stay stock still.

He pulls back when he realizes I'm not responding to his kiss. His blue eyes, which I once thought I loved—or maybe it was when I was high that I loved them—lock with mine.

"Tell me you love me too, Lissie." I shake my head slightly. "I'm your husband."

"No," I say, then I realize the audacity of this man. The way he thinks he can force his lips on me as if I would enjoy his kiss. For a man with a limp dick that can only get up for porn, he sure is cocky. "I don't want to be here anymore, with you." I breathe the words out, and then I feel the wind knocked out of me, literally, not just figuratively. His fist slams straight into my stomach, and I fall forward, my head hitting his shoulder.

"You love me, or have you forgotten?" he snarls.

I vowed the minute his hands touched me in violence, I would leave him.

I will *not* go back on my word.

Not this time.

I hold my stomach and step back, and his eyes track my movements.

"I own you, Lissie. Did you forget?" he growls,

his voice dripping with menace. His eyes bore into mine, leaving no doubt about the intensity of his claim. *Arrogant asshole!*

I turn, clutching my stomach, and head toward the door. As I twist the handle on the door, he grabs me, yanks me back, and slams the door shut.

"Where do you think you're going?"

I lick my lips, still trying to catch my breath.

He turns me with a forceful hand on my shoulder until I'm facing him. "Lissie, answer me."

"I'm leaving," I state.

"I'll send those videos to Savannah's department. I'll send them all," he threatens with a smile on his face.

"Send them," I say with clenched teeth and try to walk past him. He stops me with a hit to the back of my head, and as twinkling appears before my eyes, it's not long before everything goes black.

Chapter 10

Milo

"Do you even know her..."

"**Y**ou did what I told you *not* to do," Rebecca says as she strides into the club-house the following week.

"Yes. I did what needed to be done." I smile at her, but the smile is strained, not reaching my eyes, and for a moment, there is tense silence between us.

"Fucking hell, Milo." She shakes her head. "Your father—"

"Let's stop right there. I couldn't give two shits what that old fuck would have done. This place was a shitshow because of him. I make more money in one fucking day than he ever did in his lifetime here."

"It's not *all* about the money." I turn my gaze to her.

"So are you saying I should cut your pay?" Her face goes white at my words.

"No, of course not. I was just referring to life… it's not all about money."

"Maybe in your dream life, but in this one, the reality, it's all about the fucking money," I remind her.

She nods, and Morris sees her out. There is nothing to be gained by speaking any more words with her.

"Milo." I turn to Letti when she says my name. She makes me a coffee and places it in front of me. "Can I ask you something?" She fidgets with a spoon as I nod. "Lissie. How is she? I mean, what type of person is she now?" I look at her, confused, my brows pulling together tightly, not knowing where this conversation is going.

"I knew her in school, then she got married and no one really knows anything about her now. She has this allure about her, where she's closed off, and you are too afraid to ask for more." My lips tug at the description of her. "I think she is the prettiest woman I have ever seen. It baffles me why she is married to *that man*." She shakes her head.

Me and you both.

Letti is beautiful, and while I can appreciate her

beauty, I would never go there. We grew up together, and she is basically a sister to me. When my life got to be too much, I would end up at their house.

"Anyway, I was just wondering... do you think she would be down for a friend?" she asks.

Does Elizabeth have friends? I'm not even sure.

"Why are you asking me?"

Her eyes go wide. "I just figured you might know something since you're the only person she spends time with. I only ever see you with her."

That's because I force her to be with me.

Fuck, I wish she would give it to me freely.

I'm fucking obsessed with the woman.

And she has no idea.

"Ask her," I tell her, and then walk away.

She's late. *Again.* She missed our last session, and I don't want to miss this one.

I press call on her contact because I need to hear her voice. The way she reads does things to me.

Chapter 11

Lissie

"Sometimes love is broken."

My *head hurts.* That's the first thing I think as my eyes open. And I hear music.

I try to sit up and realize my hands won't move. Are they restrained? And this isn't my bed. Cody has me tied up in his room. I pull at my wrists, but the rope doesn't budge.

It burns my skin, and I know it will leave marks.

The sound of loud giggling filters into the room over the music, and I know his women are here. *He brought them into our house and left me tied to the bed.* I try to free my hands again, but it's no use, so I flop back to the mattress.

Fuck.

What did I do to get myself into this position?

Into this life? And how the fuck do I get myself out of it? Why can't I get myself out of it?

"Cody!" I shout his name. No one answers, and the giggling doesn't stop. "Cody!" I shout again. Tugging at my wrist, I try to pull it free from the rope.

His sheets smell like him.

Actually, the whole fucking room smells like him. Tangy, like he hasn't washed in days.

I hate the way he smells—a rancid, sour, pungent mixture of stale bullshit and asshole behavior. His scent is suffocating and makes me recoil in disgust.

I hate the way he talks—an exercise in irritation and condescension. His tone is smug, and it makes my skin crawl.

Fuck, I hate everything about him.

And now, with what he's done, I know no matter what, I will not stay in the same fucking house as this man ever again once I am able to free myself from his clutches.

"Cody!" I scream as the song ends.

The giggling stops, but the music starts again, only this time even louder.

He heard me and turned that shit up.

What a *fucking asshole.*

I lie there, listening to the god-awful music.

Pulling on the ropes, even though I can feel them cutting into my skin. I don't care—the pain is only a small distraction to the fact I'm restrained to a bed and don't know what the fuck is going to happen to me.

"Cody, let me the fuck out!"

The music is turned up louder, and I can no longer hear the girls giggling. Huffing out a breath, I scan what I can see of Cody's room. Firstly, he needs to clean in here. He has clothes strewn all over the place, and his bedspread is old and disgusting.

Kicking the metal footboard of his stupid bed, I hope it makes a loud enough sound to be heard over the music, but it just gives off a dull thud. *Shit.*

Just as I think about breaking my own wrists in order to free myself—not even sure if that will work —the door is thrown open and then quickly closes again. I know it's him before I even turn my head in that direction. He stands next to the bed and looks down at me.

His eyes, which I once loved, stare at me with hatred.

"I love you, Lissie. You get that, right?" he says, but his rigid stance and the drink held tightly in his hand tell me otherwise. His eyes are narrowed, and his mouth is set in a hard line. "You just needed to play along. We were in a rough patch. I was working to get us out of it." He shakes his head. "I love you," he says again as if he's trying to make himself believe it.

I don't believe it.

I will *never* believe his words.

"Untie me, Cody."

"No," he says and shakes his head.

"Untie me, Cody."

"No, because you are my wife, Lissie, and you will remain my wife."

"We've been in a loveless marriage for years, and what? You really expect me to stay?"

He throws his hands up, his drink spilling all over me when he pulls them down. "Yes, because that's what marriage is about... us being a team and working through things." His words make me angry. The man is clearly drunk and possibly even high.

"A real husband would not sell their wife to bikers to pay a debt *he... fucking... owes!*" I scream.

He cracks his neck, then lifts his drink to his lips and takes a sip. "I'm in this debt because of your sister," he reminds me, throwing the rest of his drink on me.

I turn my face as the cold liquid hits my skin. The alcohol stings my eyes, but I'm too damn angry to care. "Lies," I growl as the drink drips down my face. "I had money... a *lot* of it. *You* wasted it all." He leans down so close he's breathing in my face, and I can smell the alcohol permeating from his putrid mouth and pores.

"You smoked it, shot it into your veins, and drank it just as much as I did. What happened to you, Lissie? We were such a good team until you decided you were better than me."

"I *am* better than you," I throw back.

And while I was low, he took advantage of that.

Thankfully, I never became addicted. I realized when I saw a girl overdose at a party, I had to stop, or I would end up the same way. It took my sister a little longer to come to the same realization.

"You think you are, but here you lie, tied to my bed, where you belong." He scrunches up his nose, turns, and walks out. Just as I think he'll leave, he spins around and comes back to the bed. He lays his hand on my hair and brushes it from my face, then he leans down and goes to kiss my lips. I turn my face so he can't touch them, which makes him mad, and he forces my face back to his. When his mouth touches mine, I open up and bite his bottom lip. He screams, and I smile up at him.

"Don't fucking touch me again," I seethe.

He wipes his mouth with the back of his hand, his eyes wide, and when he pulls it away, he sees blood there.

"You are my wife," he says.

"You are my soon-to-be ex-husband," I snap. "Now... *Let. Me. Go.*"

"No," he says with finality. And this time, when he turns to leave, he doesn't stop or turn back around.

"Let me out, you piece of shit!" The scream dies on my lips as the music is turned up louder. And before I can stop myself, I feel the tears welling my eyes.

Why did it take me so long to leave? Yes, it was fear for my sister and the need to protect her. *But who is protecting me?*

Why am I always the last thought in everyone else's life?

When will someone put me first?

I want to be first in so many ways.

Yet here I am, last again.

Crying, tied to a bed that I haven't slept in for over two years, and held prisoner by my husband.

My fucked-up, drugged-up husband.

I don't know what time it is.

I've been stuck in the same position, unable to move, and in and out of sleep. The last thing I want to do is sleep, but my eyes are so heavy I've been dozing off and waking with a start. The music has finally died off, and I don't hear anyone around.

I call Cody's name at least three times and get nothing in response. My wrists are aching. My body keeps cramping from being stuck in the same position for so long, and I'm not even going to mention how full my bladder is. I'm not sure what else I can do because no one would care if I went missing. *Would it matter to anyone?* Yes, my sister would be upset, but she will go on with her life. The only person I've really had since my mother passed away is Cody, and he knows that and has used it to his every single advantage.

Closing my eyes, I try to think of ways to get out of this. *Should I sweet-talk him and tell him everything will be okay? Is that my only hope?*

If I have to, I will, but I have a feeling he won't believe anything I say.

The door creaks open, and I swing my head toward it, thinking Cody has come back, but I see a glimpse of blond hair. Is she one of the women who's usually here? To be honest, I don't pay attention to the women he brings home. After the first few times, it became a regular occurrence, and my care factor has nosed to nothing.

She steps in and shuts the door behind her, bringing her finger to her mouth and telling me to be quiet. I don't make a sound. I simply watch as she creeps, ever so slowly, to the head of the bed. I can smell she's been drinking, and her eyes are glassy. With shaky hands, she starts to undo the rope tying my wrists to the bed, and I crane my neck to watch her. The woman struggles at first, but she stays quiet, and I'm hoping and praying that she gets it undone.

The second my first hand is free, a sense of relief washes through me. She steps away and moves around to the other side of the bed, then starts to untie the other hand, which goes a lot faster. Immediately, I sit up when the rope falls away—my body screaming at me in pain. She steps back and offers me a small smile.

"I'm friends with Letti, and she asked if I had seen you," she whispers.

Letti. I see her often at Milo's compound but hardly talk to her.

"Thank you," I whisper and swing my legs off the bed. They are sore and shaky, but I have to take this opportunity. She nods to the window, and I turn to it.

"Cody's asleep. I've been waiting for him to pass out. I'm going to go back out there and go to sleep. Please be quiet," she says.

"What's your name?" I ask. Her smile is sad, and she shakes her head.

"You don't—"

"Please. What's your name?"

Her lipstick is smudged on her lips, and her eyes are full of worry as she pins me with them. At first, I don't think she'll answer, but then...

"Marie." She looks back over her shoulder and turns to open the door. I wait until it's shut and hurry to the window. I don't even think about going to my room to get anything. Pushing open the window, the cold morning breeze hits my skin. It stings my wrists, but I don't care. I *will not* stay in this room a second longer than necessary. Climbing out, I don't shut the window. I just run. Down the street and away from that house.

I have absolutely no idea where I'm going to go or how I'm going to get there, but I know for a fact that I'm not turning back and going into that house so he can do the exact same thing to me again.

My legs eventually get tired, and I have to slow

down. I've managed to get a few streets away from him, heading toward the center of town, when I hear my name being called.

Swinging my head around, I see Letti. She pulls over next to me and jumps out of her car.

"Marie messaged me. Are you okay?" she says, concerned.

I can't remember more than three words I've ever spoken to this woman, but I have never been more thankful in my life to see her face, and I hope she won't hurt me.

"Come. I have a spare bed. Please, I need to clean those wrists up." Letti reaches for me, and I pull away from her. She then puts her hands up to show she has nothing in them and means me no harm. "I'm sorry. I just want to help. Do you have somewhere else to go? Someone I can perhaps call?"

My sister? No, I don't want to call her.

"Should we go to the police?" she asks, and I shake my head. If the police rocked up to his house, he would for sure show the video of Savannah.

"No," I reply.

"Okay, it's just me in a small apartment. It's not much, but it is home." She shrugs. "I have a spare room. You could always stay there until you find somewhere."

Her offer is so kind—I'm not used to good people.

"Why are you helping me?"

"I think you need it. I mean, I could be wrong, but you have this lost look in your eyes, and when I didn't see you this week at the clubhouse, I asked around."

"Thank you," I whisper, and she offers me the kindest smile.

I wonder if this is how it feels to have someone care about you.

Someone with no ulterior motives and under no conditions.

Chapter 12

Milo

"What use is a finger if you cut it off?"

It's now been three weeks since I've seen *her*. The second week, Cody made excuses, and I knew he was fucking lying. She isn't my wife, so it's not my job to question the choices of her husband, but fuck, I sure as shit want to put my fist through his face.

"Do you plan to just sit there?" Morris asks Aiden, who is watching with wide eyes as Morris cuts off a guy's finger while the guy's screams fill the shed.

"No, no." Aiden rushes over. He's wearing gloves, the kind hairdressers use, and his face is pale. Morris lifts the finger he chopped off and holds it out to him.

"You do know what to do with this, don't you?"

Morris raises a brow at Aiden. I hear a chuckle and turn around to see Axe walk in. I'm tall, but Axe has my six foot-three beat. He's close to seven feet.

"You're back," Morris yells to him.

Axe sits next to me and ignores Morris. "It's a mess," he says to me. "You made a mess. And I cleaned it up."

"Good." I turn back to see Aiden start to sway as he holds the finger.

Axe is our enforcer, and he was off cleaning up a mess that I may or may not have made. If you'd just met him, you would think he's one scary mother-fucker. And while he is that, he is also one of the calmest-headed guys I have ever met.

When I want to go off the deep end, he tries to pull me back. Even if I don't listen half the time, and when I don't listen, he will join me. He's loyal—as good to me as Morris is.

When my father died and I took over, I killed two of his men. They said I wasn't fit for this life, that I would ruin everything they worked so hard to build. Then I went and made it better, with better men.

My father's men were disloyal, stealing products and money whenever they could. Doing deals on the side that didn't benefit the club.

Everything we do now benefits the club.

We don't just run the biggest drugs racket in this city; we run the biggest in the fucking state. We also own many businesses in this shithole of a town that I grew up in. I know most people by name. And if I don't? Well, they aren't worthy of my fucking time. But then again, no one is.

"I think he's about to faint," Axe says, and I lift my head to see Aiden sway even more. "Should we make a bet?" Axe yells out to Morris.

"No, fucker, he's about to go down," Morris says, pointing at Aiden.

"I am not..." Aiden trails off just before he falls. We all stand there watching as he drops to the floor. The dealer in Morris's chair is passed out cold—pain does that to you when it's too much to handle. Obviously, it was too much for him.

"Where has your little bird been?" Axe asks, looking at me.

"How would you know she hasn't been around? You've been gone for weeks," I say.

Then it hits me. "Mason," I mumble, and he nods.

Screams echo through the shed, and we all look at the man tied to the chair as he thrashes about like a fucking idiot. *Like that will get him anywhere.*

"Are you finally off the drug dealer's wife?" Axe asks.

"He owes me."

"And I'm sure she's paid his debt to you by now."

She has, but I'm not willing to tell that fucking sleazebag that. Cody will do as I fucking say.

"Why do you care?" Axe turns his gaze to Morris, who is currently kicking Aiden to wake him the fuck up.

"You like her," Axe states. "You don't like anyone. You fuck women, sure, but you never see them more than a few times. So why her, especially since she is married?"

"Do you think I care that she's married? Do you think I care what any of you think about who I fuck or spend my time with?" I stand, and he shakes his head.

"Get him the fuck up." I point to Aiden. "Do your job and stop worrying about who I invite into my fucking house."

Axe nods.

And Morris grumbles something as Aiden wakes up, the finger still clutched in his hand.

"Clean this shit up," I order as I stalk off.

Chapter 13

Lissie

"To get a job?"

Letti has been amazing. She's made me feel welcome and not so much like a victim the way I've felt for the last few years. It's nice to have someone check on you to see that you are okay. And the kicker? They want nothing in return.

That feeling is so unlike anything I've known.

"I think I need a job. I need to..." I let the words rush out so quickly my brain can't finish the thought. "I can't stay here and expect you to support me."

"It's only been two weeks, Lissie. You haven't asked for anything; you cook, you clean. Hell, you can live here as long as you want. It saves me from doing everything." She laughs. "But for real, I appreciate what you've been doing."

How weird and funny is it that she appreciates me for cleaning and cooking for her? The first three days I was here, I stayed locked in her spare room, just lying there, wondering what I was going to do. I snuck out and stole some bread on the second day. On the third, she was waiting for me. She offered me food, and I sat with her in silence as we ate. She never pressured me to talk to her or to tell her what happened.

I told her on the fourth day.

That day, she came home with more food.

The day after that, I cooked and cleaned while she was out working.

"I've never really had anyone before, apart from Cody. So I'm not really sure what to say or do, but I want a job," I tell her.

"Okay, let's find you one. What experience do you have so we know where to look first?"

I sit back on the stool in her kitchen and stare at her. *How do I tell her?* My only job has been reading to the president of the motorcycle club, which I'm not sure she knows about. Actually, I'm not sure anyone knows that I read to him. They know that I work for him, but maybe they think I'm in there fucking him.

"Do you think I'm a whore?" I ask.

Her eyes go wide, and she shakes her head. "Oh my God, no. Why would you say that?"

"You know I see Milo. What do you think I do for him?"

She bites her lip as her gaze darts around the room and then finally comes back to me. "To be honest, we never really asked. For the simple fact that it's Milo." She shrugs.

"Did you think I was sleeping with him?"

"What? No, of course not."

"Why not?"

"Because you're married."

"Married people cheat on their spouses all the time," I tell her.

"But not you," she says, and I nod. "Look, we all know what an ass Cody is. Everyone knew he was lucky to have you..." She pauses. "I can ask the club about a job," she offers. "Morris is my brother. I'm sure he'll know if there's something you could help out with."

Just as she finishes, a knock comes on the door. I freeze as she stands. Without a second thought, she walks to the door and pulls it open. Morris stands there with a bag of groceries that he hands her, and then his gaze lands on me and narrows.

"What's Prez's pet doing in your kitchen?" he asks Letti.

"Pet?" I say, baffled.

"Yes, that's what you are. His pet."

I turn away from him.

Pet.

Is this what my life has come to, being a man's pet?

"That's a mean thing to say, Morris. *Apologize. Now*," Letti scolds.

"She comes, they go into his room, they don't fuck. And then she leaves. We all know she ain't in his room cleaning."

"How would you know that?" Letti asks, and a small piece of me feels better knowing she's sticking up for me, even though she has no idea why I go and see him.

"Letti..." Morris starts.

"Don't *Letti* me. Thanks for the food, but you can go now. Come back when you're ready to speak to my friend with some respect." She shuts the door in his face, and I smile brightly.

As a teenager, I always thought I had a backbone, but then I lost my mother. And then I was with Cody. And somehow, everything kind of shifted and changed along the way.

I want to be the same person I had hoped to be. But I just don't know how.

Milo is at the door later that day, and it takes me by surprise. I swing my head around to stare at him. He's dressed in his leather and looking way too good.

"Letti," Milo says, his gaze shifting to me where I sit on Letti's couch. She was watching some reality TV show that she's obsessed with, and I'm here for moral support.

"Elizabeth," he says, using my full name. "A word, if you wouldn't mind."

I get up from the couch and move to stand in front of him. Just as I reach him, his hand shoots out and grabs my wrists. "How did you get these marks?" he growls. I look down to where the rope burns are etched into my skin. They are fully healed now, and only an angry red mark is left. *How did he see that so quickly?* I pull my hands away from his grasp and tuck them behind me.

"I'll go to my room. Call out if you need me," Letti says.

"She won't need you," Milo answers for me.

I stay where I am, blocking the doorway, not inviting him inside.

"Why are you not at home? And where is your husband?" he asks, his head tilting to the side.

"I left him."

A slight smirk touches his lips before it's replaced with a scowl, and he asks again, "How did you get the marks?" I look back down at my wrists.

"Know of any jobs available?" I ask, changing the subject. Why is it that I know Milo is way more dangerous than Cody, but I feel safer with him?

"A job?" he asks, surprised. His hands slide into his pockets, and he leans against the doorjamb. "You have a job. You work for me."

"Okay, how much are you paying me? We need to renegotiate." His lips fight a smirk. "Don't laugh, I need things. I left with nothing," I say angrily.

His smirk drops, and he steps in closer to me. "Come on, we can discuss this on the way."

"What? Where?" I ask, afraid of leaving this nice safe haven I have created for myself.

"You need things, and we can discuss a job opportunity and new wages once I take you shopping."

"I'm not going shopping with you." I cross my

arms over my chest. I mean, why would I? Does he think I'm a charity case? Because I'm *not*.

"Letti," he calls out. Her door opens, and she steps out. "Helmet," he demands, and I turn to look at her.

"He forgot to say please," I say. She just smiles and walks back into her room. I feel his breath on my neck before he speaks.

"I will say please to one woman only." I spin around to look at him. "Let's go, or I'll carry you again."

Carry me? When did he... *oh, to his bed the night I fell asleep outside the clubhouse.* He nods and heads outside.

"Here you go," Letti says, handing me a helmet. "I don't wear it much, so it's basically brand new." I take it from her.

"Should I stay here? I should stay, right?" I ask, hoping she'll say yes. I shouldn't get on a bike with a man who is known for killing people.

"I think you should go," she says. "If you're comfortable with it."

I am. I don't feel like I'm in any danger around Milo.

Nodding my head, I carry the helmet out to where he's waiting for me with his bike.

He is wearing his leather jacket and black jeans, and his hair is slicked back. Damn, he looks good. He would give Jax Teller a run for his money any day. Grabbing his helmet, he motions to the one in my hand. "Put it on."

I stand there as he pulls his helmet on and straddles the bike.

He turns to me. "Do you need a hand getting on?"

"I'm sure I shouldn't be getting on this thing," I say. He leans the bike over so I don't have to lift my leg too high, then shakes his head at my discomfort as I continue to stand there. Then he kicks his bike to a stand and gets off. I'm confused at first until he lifts me bridal style, being careful of where his hands are, and puts me on the back of the bike. I say nothing as he gets on, and I put my hands on his sides.

"Hands here." He taps my hands and pulls them around to his front. "Hold on."

I was never a fan of bikes growing up. Cody always said there was never any good that came from them, and who was I to argue with him?

The bike slows down as we near the shopping center, and as he comes to a stop, we both sit there for a moment.

"Don't move." His hand touches mine, where

they rest on his stomach. He gives me a small squeeze before he pulls my hands away and gets off the bike. I sit there watching him as he removes his helmet. He then pulls mine off with ease before leaning down and lifting me up again.

People stare.

They always do when Milo is involved.

"I could have done that myself," I tell him. Granted, I've never been on a bike before, but I'm sure I could get off easily enough if I tried.

"If you say so. Though you did look like a deer in headlights trying to work out how to sit on it without touching me," he says with a raised brow.

"Why does your vest say President?" I ask, tapping the patch on his chest. When he turns around, his club's logo is on the back of it.

He places both our helmets on the bike. No one in this town would be stupid enough to steal from anyone in the club. "What do you think it means?" he asks. He slips one hand into his pocket as we walk toward the shops. Parents pull their kids in a little tighter to their sides when they pass us, but Milo doesn't seem to notice or care.

"I take it you don't come to the shops often?" I say, looking around at everyone who forgot their manners today.

"No," he answers, peering down at me.

"I think it means you run the club. But how?"

"You know it was my father's club, yes?" I did know that much, but I always thought someone else would take over when the old man died. "When he died, it became mine."

"Ohhh. Is that how it usually works?"

"No, but he made it clear to everyone that was how it was going to be, and everyone respected him."

"Do they respect you?"

"You sure are asking a lot of questions today, Elizabeth."

I shrug in response before asking, "Why are you taking me shopping?"

"You need things, and it's payment for our next reading session."

"So, you *are* going to pay me?"

The corner of his lip lifts in a smirk, and he locks eyes with me.

"I guess so."

"Why would you offer to pay me?" I pressure him. We stop out front of a women's shop, and he keeps those eyes pinned on me. "Cody gets that money, not me."

"Well now you will get it and because I know

pain. And even though pain likes to fester by itself, yours shouldn't."

I don't know what to say to that. Why does this man think I'm worthy of his time when my husband thinks so low of me?

I turn and walk into the shop, and he follows close behind me. After picking a few things that I need, I head to the fitting room. Milo sits on one of the sofas in front as I step into the tiny cubicle. I slide my clothes off before I reach for the dress on the hanger. It's a black maxi dress that is loose around my stomach and comfortable enough to get around in. Reaching for the zipper, I realize I can't zip it up on my own. I think about taking it off, but when I look in the mirror, I love it. Luckily, it's half price, so I wouldn't be spending much on it with whatever he will pay me. And I do desperately need my own clothes.

Cody hated me in dresses, not that I complained about my clothes. I had some nice pieces, all of which were approved by him.

Deciding to ask a sales lady for help, I open the door to see Milo, one ankle propped on his other knee, his foot shaking. The sales lady next to him is leaning down as she talks to him, her tits on full display.

Milo spots me straight away, but she keeps talking, not even noticing me.

I cough to gain her attention.

She looks my way and stands straight as if she's guilty of something.

"Is this your girlfriend, Milo? You never dated any of us back in school." She smiles at me, but it's forced and a little catty.

"I need help with the dress," I say deadpan, ignoring them both and turning around to show the back. I feel it gets zipped slowly, and when I turn my head to thank her, I see Milo standing there.

"What do you think?" I ask him, looking down at the dress. His gaze doesn't leave mine for a few heartbeats, and then it tracks down my dress.

"It's not really your color if you want an honest opinion. We could find something else," the sales lady says.

Who even says something like that?

I glare at her as Milo says, "It's perfect."

I spin around and tap my shoulder, indicating for him to unzip it. He does, and without a thank you, I step back into the changing room and pull off the dress.

Then he buys it for me.

Perfect.

Chapter 14

Milo

"Meet the family."

Jill stands in front of me, her eyes kind as she takes me in.

"You haven't been around," she says, then turns her attention to Elizabeth, who has been silent since we walked out of that shop and I bought her the dress. "Hi." Elizabeth smiles at her, and Jill looks back at me, waiting for an answer.

"I've been busy." Her hand lands on my arm and squeezes it.

"Come and visit, please?" Jill says.

I glance at Elizabeth, whose eyes are pinned on Jill's hand where she touches me.

"I'll just go to the bathroom and let you two talk," Elizabeth says.

"Stay," I tell her.

"I'm Jill." Jill offers Elizabeth her hand, and she takes it.

"I'm Lissie. Milo is free all day. He just has to drop me off at home first, right?" She smiles big, dropping Jill's hand, and turns back to me. I grind my teeth. "He said he was free all day to take me shopping, and I got a dress, so I think that's a win. Please, you take him."

Take me? What the fuck am I, some kind of puppy?

"You can come?" Jill asks me, happiness evident in her tone.

"I'll bring Elizabeth with me," I say, glaring down at the little traitor.

"Thanks," Jill gushes, looking from Elizabeth back to me. "We've missed you. You're a hard man to convince to come to events, you know," she says, then thanks Elizabeth again before she walks off.

"Why on earth would you want me to go to your girlfriend's house?" Elizabeth asks when Jill is out of hearing range.

"That isn't my girlfriend." I lean down. "And why would you do that? Do you think I'm not busy?"

"Who is she, then? And no, of course, you aren't busy if you have time to take me shopping. Cody never did." She throws that last bit in, and we let those words hang between us.

"She's my aunt," I say, clearing up the confusion.

"Oh…" Her cheeks blush red. "And your mother?" she asks.

"Died when I was a teenager. It's why I stayed in this shithole of a city, as you like to call it. It wasn't because of my fucked-up father, that's for sure."

"I'm sorry. I didn't know." She averts her gaze.

"It's fine. But if I have to deal with that, thanks to you, you're coming, too."

"Shouldn't you take your girlfriend, not me, to meet your family?" she asks, shaking her head.

"I don't have a girlfriend. I have women I fuck. Do you want to be on that list?"

She rears back as if my words physically slapped her. "Fuck off, Milo." She turns and storms off.

Well, shit, look at her go.

I follow and spin her back toward me with a hand on her arm. "Just because you let that piece of shit treat you like garbage doesn't mean you should let anyone else do it." Her hand lifts, and she slaps me hard across the face. I smile down at her. People around us stop to stare.

"I don't want a lift home from you. I'll take a cab or walk," she seethes as she reaches for the bag I'm holding. But I don't let it go. We're drawing a crowd —I can feel their stares penetrating my back, but I keep a hold of her bag.

"Elizabeth," I growl, then go quiet for a moment. "I apologize."

Her eyes go wide, and she looks at me, really looks at me. Those big, beautiful fucking eyes haunt me, and I think about her words that sing me off to a fucking slumber every night. Her smell is still embedded in my sheets, and I refuse to wash them.

"I—"

"You don't have to go with me if it pains you that much to be around me," I tell her. "Let's get you home."

Chapter 15

Lissie

"I've never had a man apologize to me before and mean it."

Milo Savage is many things, but someone who apologizes to women? I didn't think that was possible.

I'm learning so much about him.

"Milo," I say his name softly as he walks off with my bag, but he hears me anyway. When he turns back, his eyes lock on mine and hit me hard. So hard, but I try not to look away. I bet many people do when he looks at them like that. They're intense, and it's as if they can eat into your soul with just a simple glance. It's then I realize how dark his chocolate eyes are. His lashes are full and thick, and when he closes his eyes, they rest on perfectly sculpted cheekbones.

"I'll go with you," I tell him.

He gives a quick jerk of his head in acknowledgment, and we head over to his bike. He helps me with my helmet, strapping it under my chin before he straddles his ride. After his own helmet is in place on his head, he glances back at me, waiting for me to get on behind him. I don't take his offered hand or let him think he can pick me up again. I get on with little help, wrapping both arms around his waist. He grunts once before he takes off, the bike's engine roaring. I plaster myself to his back, closer than I was last time, as he rides.

It doesn't take long before he pulls up to an unfamiliar house. He gets off and wastes no time before lifting me up and helping me off. I wince, and he looks at me, confused.

"Milo, you came." He turns toward Jill as she approaches. I can't help but stare at Milo. He's tall, with tightly packed muscles. Nothing like Cody. Cody is taller than me, but he was lean and built like a runner at the beginning before he got hooked on drugs and whatever else he was into. "And you brought your friend. Come inside. Everyone is here already. As soon as they heard the news you were coming, they wanted to say hi. It's not every day you come over to visit the family."

Milo gives me a look over his shoulder before he follows Jill inside. I step up next to him as we walk through the white door leading into the house. It's your average one-story home, but you can feel the love as soon as you enter. The cozy living room welcomes us with its soft lighting and comfortable furniture. Pictures line the walls, capturing memories and happy moments. The sound of giggles echoes from the other rooms, creating an inviting atmosphere that envelops me instantly.

"Cassy, come say hello to Milo and his friend." A teenager with the same hair as Milo—dark with lighter strands throughout—comes around the corner. She stands tall and smiles when she sees him. The giggling stops, then starts again, and Jill puts an arm around the girl's shoulders. "Milo, you remember my oldest, Cassy. The other two are in the kitchen, also giggling if you can't hear them. And your uncle is out back, barbecuing."

"We already ate," Milo says, and Jill's smile drops.

"Well, if you're hungry, feel free to eat." She waves us through as Cassy stares at me.

"She's really pretty, Milo." Her soft eyes are on me before she turns to Milo, and I see she admires him. "Is she your girlfriend?"

"No, she's married," he mumbles, causing her eyes to widen.

"Hi," I reply. "Milo was nice enough to take me to the shops."

Jill turns back then and looks at us.

"That's nice of you," Cassy says. "And you aren't all that nice, Milo."

Jill scolds her daughter and tells her to go away while I giggle.

Milo glares at me.

"What?" I ask innocently.

"I'm not nice?" he asks, knowing what I'm laughing at.

I shrug. "It's the truth." I smirk before I follow Jill. Milo falls in behind me until we reach the kitchen, where the forest-green backdoor opens, and a man steps inside. He has a kind smile.

"Uncle Lester." Milo nods.

Lester wraps his arms around Milo and pats him on the back. "Been too long, kid. Way too long."

"He's too busy being scary to see us," Cassy adds with the perfect eye roll.

I wonder if I was like that as a teenager.

"Scary? Is that what you are?" I ask Milo as his uncle releases him and stands proudly next to him.

"Some would assume so," Milo grumbles as his eyes narrow at me.

My lips thin as I try to hide my smile.

"Seems you don't think so," Lester says.

"Milo is just a big teddy bear," I tell them. "And he has issues with personal space," I add, referring to that time I woke up in his bed.

"Just yours," Milo mutters under his breath.

I ignore him and turn to Lester. "Are you Milo's mother's brother?"

"Yes, dear." He pauses, then addresses Milo. "You've told her about your mother?"

Milo watches me as he speaks, "She knows she died. That's it." And he leaves it at that.

Jill hums loudly before she turns and goes back to cooking whatever she was making before we arrived.

"How did she die?" I ask, and everyone goes quiet at my question.

"On the back of my father's bike," Milo says. He's being vague, but the pain I see in his expression tells me to drop it. On a good day, Milo doesn't use a lot of his words. I doubt I'll get him to tell me something that's painful for him.

"It's been almost a year since you've visited," Cassy says, breaking the awkward silence.

"I'm busy," Milo replies without a care in the world.

Lester nods. "They say the club is better than it's ever been."

"Yes, it is," Milo states.

"Proud of you." Lester claps him on the back.

"You never wanted me to join," Milo points out, and I can hear a bit of anger in his tone.

"Yes, but you're like your mother and do what you want. So I'm glad you're turning it around for the better."

"Lissie, do you hang out at the club often? Milo won't let me go," Cassy asks.

"A little, yeah." Milo grinds his teeth at my answer. "But not lately."

I observe him as he interacts with them, and it's not the same way he is with me. I can tell he knows these people, but he's still reserved, not that he isn't with me. Except when Milo looks at me, I feel like he sees more of me as I do him.

Cassy makes small talk with me for a good hour before Milo stands and tells them we have to go. As we walk out and he hands me my helmet, I turn to face him. "It must be nice to have people who love and care about you." Milo doesn't respond. He simply puts his helmet on and climbs onto his bike.

I don't know much about my father—as far as I know, he died when I was young. All I had was my mother, and I saw Savannah on holidays. So I don't understand why he doesn't appreciate the family he has.

I climb onto the bike easier this time. Milo reaches back, grabs my hands, and pulls them tight around his chest. He holds one hand there as he starts the bike. I lean my head against his back. He smells of leather and so *many* possibilities.

"Did you really think I wouldn't get you to work sooner rather than later?" Milo says as he walks into the apartment the next day. I'm curled up on the couch, wearing the dress he bought me and reading a book I started last night and haven't been able to put down, thanks to Letti and her extensive book collection.

"What?" I ask. I sigh as I lay the book down on my chest. Dammit! I just got to a really good part. He picks up the book and scans the page as his frame takes up all my air and space. He's dressed in his leathers and smells just as good as he usually does.

He lets out a haughty laugh before those dark eyes find mine.

"He slides it in, nice and slow, hitting every spot imaginable." He stops reading aloud, glances at me, and returns to the book, picking up where he left off. *"He's a God in the bedroom, the way he slips one hand behind my head and grips my hair while the other hand finds its way to my core."* He stops again and raises a brow. "Do you know what a core is?" I'm too stunned to speak because of the way he just read, which has me squeezing my legs a little tighter together. *Why was that so hot? Is this how he feels when I read to him?*

"Elizabeth." I don't even know what he's saying. When I don't answer, he looks back to the book. *"His hand plays with me like he's been playing delicate music all his life and it's waited for the right chord to pluck—my chord—and oh my god, talk about build-up. His hands hold me still. His body weight is heavy, and his..."* My eyes are closed as he reads, and when they spring open at the sudden silence, I see him studying me. "You enjoy this." I nod. No shame in it. Romance is for everyone. Men watch porn because they are usually more stimulated by visuals, while women prefer to create the perfect scenarios in their minds.

Who knew this was my perfect scenario?

"Elizabeth, if you don't—"

My hand slides between my legs. I just need a little pressure. But as I touch myself with Milo watching, I realize I need more than a *little* pressure. His tongue darts out of his mouth and licks that scar I love. There is definitely something to be said about touching yourself with a man who exudes sex appeal from his pores while watching you. I work hard to keep my hips steady while I maintain eye contact with him.

"You can go now," I say, smiling.

"So you can fuck yourself?" He scoffs. His eyes leave mine and stray back to my hand, playing between my legs. "I can see you applying pressure. Do you need help?" He shows me his hand that isn't holding the book, and I shake my head.

He smirks.

"Bye, Milo," I breathe out.

He looks pained at first, but then he takes my book with him when he leaves. And the first thing I do is run to my room and touch myself for real, with Milo's face front and center in my mind. Even when I try to think of something else, it's his face that dominates every image in my head.

Afterward, I realize it's the first time I have ever

felt a need, a want like that. Something I never got with my husband.

Am I cheating?

Is that what this is?

Shaking my head, I strip myself down, get in the shower, and scrub myself of my bad thoughts.

Chapter 16

Milo

"Fuck, if only I knew that was all it took."

"Y ou've been smiling all fucking day, it's sickening," Axe grumbles as he sits across from me.

"Aiden is still alive, in case you were wondering," Morris says, stepping into the room.

"I wasn't," I tell him and then look back to Axe. "And I'm not fucking smiling."

"You've been around to see her?" Morris asks.

"Who?" Axe wants to know.

Aiden walks to the bar and gets a bottle of water, then holds it against his head. He has a bump from where he fell the other day. Morris told him to carry around the finger to remind him to stop being a bitch.

"I have," I reply.

Morris smirks and turns to Axe. "Lissie is staying with Letti," he tells him.

"Prez." We all turn as Mason walks in. "Cody is here."

I stand before anyone else, walk out the doors and go straight to the back. I find Cody, with sunglasses covering his eyes, smoking a cigarette. Two women sit in his car as he waits for me. When he spots me, he stands a little taller.

"Milo. Hey, man." He pushes his fingers through his hair. "I have another woman, you know, to fill Lissie's shoes. You see, she ran off. Decided to find another man and ran the fuck off on me." A woman with dark hair and washed-out eyes gets out of the car, and he waves to her. "See, she will do. You can use her the same way, right?" He drops the cigarette to the ground and steps on it with his shoe before he looks up at me, pushing his sunglasses up on his head and revealing his bloodshot eyes. I feel Axe come up behind me.

"Hi," the woman says with a wave of her hand.

"Where the fuck have you been?" I ask Cody. He scratches his arm, and that tells me everything I need to know.

"Look, I've had a busy few weeks, but I've always been good with payment. What do you need for late payment? This one will suck your cock." He motions to the woman, who nods her head. "Free, of course, and you can do whatever it is you want to her."

"Fucking hell," Axe mutters behind me.

"Take your fucking whores and come back with my money," I tell him.

His gaze jumps from me to Morris and Axe, and he scratches his arm again.

"Man, I don't have it. We had a deal before, can't we just—"

I lift my gun and aim it at his head, cutting him off. "You have exactly one week to get my fucking money, or the first thing you will lose will be..." I aim the gun lower until it's pointing at his cock, savoring the terror in his eyes. I lean in closer, the tension intensifying. "You feel me, *man*?" The inflection of my voice is dangerously sarcastic, and my brow arched in sinister promise.

"This one time, Milo shot one ball off a naked man. Damn, it was amazing to watch. Painful, but the precision? Amazing," Morris says.

"I'll bring you her," he says, his voice trembling with a flicker of hope. His eyes search for any sign of mercy in my cold, hard gaze. He swallows hard, a bead of sweat trickling down his temple.

"No, that's done."

I turn and head back to the clubhouse when I hear him yell, "That fucking slut really fucked *me* over."

Pushing my gun into Axe's hand, I stalk toward Cody. When I reach him, I clock him hard, my fist flying straight into his fucking ugly mug of a face. "I'd watch how you speak about her around me," I warn, seething at him. "Now, fuck off before I decide you're better payment to me dead."

The woman scrambles into the car, as he climbs into the driver's side. Then he reverses quickly, the tires spinning on the dead grass, the tail end of the car fishtails wildly, skidding across the uneven ground. The engine wails in protest as he speeds away, his fear evident even from a distance.

"You know he ain't gonna get the money," Morris says.

"Not my fucking problem. If he comes back without the money, shoot him in the leg," I tell them, and they both nod.

Chapter 17

Lissie

"I want my book back."

The next day, Letti is washing dishes as I enter the kitchen. I'm not sure how to ask her for anything when she has already given me so much.

"I-I need a lift," I say with a slight stutter.

She raises a brow, and her hand pauses at the sink as she leans on it. "To where?" she asks with a smile on her face.

"The clubhouse." Her eyes light with mischief, a playful glint in her eyes.

"I need to head there too. Is there a reason you want to go? Dare I say it's because of Milo?" She wiggles her brows, and I mockingly laugh, but it comes out more like a nervous chuckle.

"He took my book and I want it back," I say, shaking off whatever she's insinuating.

"And does he do that often?" She looks at me, puzzled.

"No, he just..." What am I going to say? He wanted to service me? No. "I just need it. I'm bored, and that book was providing entertainment."

"Okay." She shrugs and steps past me, grabbing her keys.

I slip on my sandals and follow her out. "Do you enjoy working there?" I ask.

"Yes, though it's changed. It's cleaner now that Milo runs the place." That makes me think of his room and the pristine white bed sheets. It was so odd, but I didn't really put much thought into it.

Until now.

Now, Milo is a source of unwanted turmoil in my head. He is in there like glue that is impossible to remove.

I want to remove him.

Why? Because I'm married.

It may be a loveless marriage, and it may have been over a long time ago, but I'm still married. And even though I've left Cody, until it's official, I won't cheat on him. I won't stoop to his level.

"Cody is back," she mentions, and my body locks up in shock. "Morris told me. Just wanted you to know." I'm not sure what to say to that. I haven't seen or heard from him since I escaped, and I'm thankful for that. He is the last person I want to see, and soon, I'll have to talk to someone about getting a divorce. But I really need a job first. I need income to even begin to pay for a lawyer.

"I want you to know how thankful I am for you," I tell her. "I promise I will pay you back... for everything."

"It's no issue, really. I enjoy having company. Plus, I was going to throw all those clothes out anyway."

"You bought me new underwear," I remind her.

"Yeah, I guess you can pay me back for those if it makes you happy." She laughs, parking her car in front of the clubhouse and getting out. I climb out, too, and we walk next to each other as we head around the back. It's late, and there's a fire lit in the firepit where almost everyone is gathered.

"Lissie, that you?" I turn to see Mason holding two drinks in his hands as he walks out of the enclosed area where the bar is located. In two large steps, he has his arms around my shoulders, hugging me. "It's good to see you." He pulls away and nods to where everyone is sitting. "Come say hello."

I notice his vest no longer says "Prospect" on it. He's obviously moved up in the club. I spot Milo straight away. He has a woman next to him, but he pays her no attention as he sits there listening to something Aiden is saying. Milo's gaze, however, is trained on me. There are a few people I don't recognize, but most of them I do. It feels awkward, as I know this place is invite-only. And usually, when I'm here, I read to Milo and then leave, so there's no other socialization.

"Prez, you see Lissie is back." Mason passes Milo a drink and sits down beside him.

Milo says nothing, and everything goes quiet, but once he realizes how awkward it is, he starts talking. "Why are you here?" His voice, the only sound besides the fire crackling.

"I want my book back," I reply, straightening my shoulders to try to stand tall. I feel the eyes of his men on me.

"Why?" he asks.

"So I can read it, obviously."

He shakes his head. "That's not the real reason. Now, why do you want it back?" I grind my teeth at his stubbornness. I know what he wants to hear. "Use your words, Elizabeth. Why do you want it back?"

"Because I want to pleasure myself with all the smutty scenes I read." I place my hand on my hip, and his smirk only grows as someone whistles. He taps the small space next to him as Mason moves over. I try not to think of the flush of blood that rushes to my cheeks, knowing everyone just heard me say that.

"Sit."

Stepping through the middle of the circle, I stop when I'm standing in front of him. "Give me my book back," I demand, holding my hand out.

"Sit," he repeats, and my annoyance flares.

"Book. Now." He looks away, ignoring me.

Huffing, I turn around and walk to his bike. I know he's watching me from his spot by the fire. I lift my leg, ignoring the twinge it delivers, and kick his bike. It falls over onto its side.

People stand, gasping.

Letti calls my name.

And I think for a good second that it was a very stupid thing to do.

But I told myself I would never let a man hold me hostage or treat me that way again. Maybe I should have thought about my actions for a little longer, though, especially about where we are and who I just mightily pissed off.

Holding my ground and not backing down, I flip him the finger as I turn and stomp out to the driveway with every intention to walk my ass home or at least get far enough away so he doesn't kill me in his backyard. When I reach the entrance to the property, it's dark, and I hug my arms around my body as I turn left on the road. I make sure to stay on the side of the road as I hear footsteps running up behind me. I turn as they reach me, ready to kick whoever it is when I'm lifted into the air.

I know that smell.

It haunts me.

In more ways than one.

"I should spank your fucking ass for touching my damn bike, let alone pushing it over." Milo walks with me, thrown over his shoulder.

"You shouldn't steal other people's property and then refuse to give it back," I shout, hitting his back, but he's not even flinching. "Put me down."

Milo carries me back to the clubhouse. He stalks past everyone, and I hear my name uttered a few times before he kicks open a door and drops me on a bed. It's bigger than the last bed, but it has white sheets like the other one. I run my hands over the sheets as my gaze tracks him in the dark. He flicks on the light, locks the door, picks up a chair, and places it in front of the door before he pulls my book out from his vest and sits facing me.

"I want my book," I insist, holding out my hand.

There's no point in trying to leave—he has the door locked, and his body is parked in front of it. He doesn't say anything as he looks down and opens to the page he has marked with a piece of paper.

"Those hands, hands that will haunt me for days and days to come, roughly stroke every inch of my body."

"Give me my book," I mutter.

He ignores me.

"I'd always imagined what those hands would feel like, taste like, even as he would slide one finger into me before he would utter sweet, dirty words to me. I breathe heavier as they move lower and lower." I realize he's read the book and gone to a different part from where I left off.

I've read this part already, but having him read it? *Fuck.*

"I'm already wet." He pauses and meets my eyes. "Are you wet, Elizabeth?"

My jaw grinds front to back as I stare at him with heated, angry eyes. "No." The lie slips easily off my tongue. I think he can taste it in the air because he clucks his tongue before he goes back to reading.

"He does that to me easily..." He pauses as someone knocks, thank God because he moves his chair and opens the door. I stand from the bed and move up behind him, trying to snatch the book back, but I'm stopped by the voice on the other side of the door.

"I didn't realize you had company," one of his men says.

Ignoring him, I turn to Milo, who's still blocking my path to leave.

I try to leave, but he catches me. Milo swears under his breath and shuts the door in whoever's face, then pushes the chair back before he resumes his seat and locks his gaze on me. "Sit. We aren't done."

I try to snatch the book back and scream, "We *are* done! I want to leave, go and fuck some whore to get this shit out of your system."

He chuckles at my outburst, shaking his head.

I turn and see a side table. Stomping over to it, I go to kick it over, but before I can, he grabs me by my hips and pulls me backward, my back slamming into his front.

"Don't kick my shit! And I don't want to fuck some whore. Not the way I would fuck you that is," he says, his breath on my neck. He turns me around, so I have to meet his glare.

"Stop pissing me off. And give me my book back. Don't you get it? It's mine. You men can't have fucking everything *that... is... mine!*" I scream. As soon as the last word is out, his lips slam down on mine. At first, I don't move because I'm shocked by what's happening, that is, until his hands start to roam up my sides, then slide back down and grab my ass. I open my mouth to say something, and that's the only invitation he needs to pull our bodies closer together. I feel him all over me, and my body responds in a manner I don't want it to.

It wants him.

Badly.

I hate my body for betraying me.

I shouldn't want him—not Milo. He is everything I shouldn't want.

A loud bang comes on the door, and I pull away to see him smirking.

"You taste good, Elizabeth." He swipes his thumb over his bottom lip, and I try to restrain myself from leaning forward and kissing him again.

Because I want to.

I enjoyed that kiss more than I should have.

Why did it taste and feel so good?

But then the anger and frustration take over again. "How dare you," I seethe, shaking my head. Stepping past him, I pull open his door to find Letti standing there.

"Take me home, *please*." She looks over my shoulder at Milo. "*He* doesn't get a say."

I hear a low chuckle from behind me as Letti nods her head and waves for me to follow her. Everyone watches as I walk out. I glance their way once and don't look back until we reach her car.

"Are you okay?" Letti asks.

I open the car door and check back to find him standing there under the moonlight.

He's so beautiful.

Deadly but beautiful.

After a moment, I turn back and scramble into the car, but I don't look back again.

I'm a bad, bad person.

And Milo Savage is a good, good kisser.

Better than my husband.

But let's face it... that would not be hard.

Chapter 18

Milo

"That kiss. Fuck my life."

I'm fucked!

Chapter 19

Lissie

**"Please stop me from dreaming of him. He
is the villain. Don't forget that."**

I'm sitting in the coffee shop waiting for Letti to finish her order when someone walks in.

When I look around it's Cody's mother who's walking in and heading straight to our table. She stops when she sees me sitting there.

"Lissie." She turns to look around. I never really had much to do with Cody's mother since she always hated me for marrying Cody so young. I've seen her only a handful of times over the years.

"I'm afraid I interrupted your coffee, but once I saw you—" She stops as she looks at me. "You don't come here often."

"No, I don't." Because Cody had all the money, I couldn't do anything.

"And your health, dear? Better? Cody said you

ran off to get better, something about being sick in the head," Cody's mother says to me. I sit there, confused. Of course, she speaks to him. And, of course, he wouldn't mention what a fuckhead *he* is or what *he* did.

"It's a shame, really," his mother says, and I don't even bother asking her what she means.

I stand, grabbing my empty purse, as Letti joins us. I turn to Cody's mother and give her a warm smile. I don't mean it, but I try not to let my discomfort show. Her eyes narrow slightly, and I feel like I see a flicker of disdain before she forces a polite smile in return.

"It was nice seeing you again. Tell my son to call me when you get home." She reaches out and grabs hold of my arm. I pull back and rub unconsciously at my wrists where Cody tied me up. They are completely healed now, but just hearing his mother talk of me *going home* to him has me feeling trapped as sure as I was when I was tied to that damn bed.

"I guess he never told you then."

"Told me what, dear?"

"That I left him for fucking his whores while he had me tied to his bed."

She blanches and takes a step back. "What an awful thing to say about my son."

"No worse than the truth."

She pats her hair. "I see what Cody meant now. You really are sick in the head."

I take a step forward. "Just because you are blind to his faults doesn't mean they aren't there."

Letti mumbles something unintelligible, so I glance back at her before she pulls me out of the shop. "Tell that dickhead to also add a bullet to his shopping list, and hopefully he can use it." I freeze at her words—suicide is a touchy subject to me. She doesn't immediately realize their impact, but I do.

And it's not her fault.

"Lissie," Letti breathes, and then her eyes go wide. "Shit, sorry. I forgot."

"It's fine. Thank you for getting me out of that situation."

"So, that's Cody's mother?" she says, changing the subject, and I don't miss the sarcastic edge in her tone.

"Yep, and I can guarantee she will be calling him right now to tell him she saw me," I say with an eye roll. "Glad I've got that interview today at that bar. What did you say it's called again? Scars?"

"Yep, and I'm sure you'll get the job." She beams at me. "Now, let's get home and get you dressed."

* * *

"They have the best steak... it's literally amazing." Letti passes me the menu as we sit in the bar. It was a great interview, and Letti wanted to stay for food. The manager was wonderful and knew I had no experience, but basically, she brushed that off and told me I could learn since it's not rocket science.

"You eat here?" I just assumed they only served alcohol.

"Yes. You haven't eaten anything good until you've tried their steak." She raises a brow at me, nodding her head at the same time. I laugh and shake mine. Lowering my gaze to the menu, I find what she mentioned—a steak with veggies on the side. A waitress comes over and takes our order, smiling at me as she does.

"You're Lissie, right? Haylee just mentioned she hired you," she says, pointing her pen at me.

"Ahhh, yeah?" I reply.

"Your next bartender," Letti says with pride.

"Always good to have new blood," she says, winking before she heads to the kitchen to put in our order.

I turn to Letti. "How do you know everyone here?"

She goes to speak as someone slides in next to me. Letti's cheeks start to pinken, and by the smell alone, I know exactly who it is. I hate that I know the way he smells and that I know without looking that he's leaning toward me.

"Because of us," he answers for her.

I still refuse to look at him, keeping my eyes locked on Letti. "Have you fucked the waitress here too?" I ask Milo, my back still to him.

"Now, Elizabeth, is that jealousy I hear?" His voice lowers to a whisper as he gets closer to my ear. "You want to fuck me?" I turn to Milo, who's watching me with eager eyes, so close that my gaze flicks to his lips. I remember how they tasted, and then I feel bad, really bad. I turn back just as the waitress comes over with our drinks and places them in front of us. Letti refuses to make eye contact with us.

"Do I get an apology for you knocking over my bike? You scratched it, Pretty Lady, and I had to get that fixed."

I ignore him and his sultry voice, which is way too close, and focus on Letti instead.

"I'll forgive you, just this once, if you'll kiss me," he croons in my ear. Letti's eyes move to Milo. I huff out a breath and turn to look at him. When I do, he wastes no time, his lips finding mine, bruising them as he kisses me.

I forget to breathe when he kisses me. It's like he sucks all my oxygen from me and takes it for himself. I'm too stunned to pull away or stop this, but thankfully—or not—he pulls away first and smirks at me. My brows shoot up, and anger hits me hard. Before I can say or do anything, he's up and leaving.

"So, you and Milo?" Stunned at what just happened, I turn back to see Letti grinning as she raises her drink toward her mouth. "We always wondered why he never settled down. Now I guess we have our answer." She takes a sip. "I mean, he always did watch you like a hawk when we were younger and you were at parties with us."

I never noticed that. But, then again, I never noticed much of anything, as I was too lost in my own pain.

"Why was he here?" I ask.

The waitress brings our steaks out, interrupting me as she places them before us, before she winks at us.

"This is on the house, girls. Enjoy. And holla at us when you're ready. The boss said you'll need something sweet after this."

"Thanks, Chastity," Lissie says as the waitress,

Chastity, walks off. I look past her and see men with leather vests, some of whom I recognize, near the pool table. I spot Mason and he holds up a beer, nodding hello to me. I don't see Milo anywhere, though.

"Who owns this place?" I ask.

"Milo does."

She cuts into her steak, and I do the same to mine. *It does look good.*

"Milo?"

"Yep. He owns a few other places, too, but I like to come here best. He hired a kid off the street and taught him how to cook. And, damn, he's a good cook."

"Milo's reputation..." I start to say.

"Oh, we all know. Most of the town is shit-scared of him, but he helped me out when no one else would. Don't get me wrong, he's scary, but the good type of scary."

"You think he's scary?"

She nods, taking a bite of steak. Her eyes close for a brief second before they open back up. "Do you not?"

"I think of him as Milo."

Just then, he walks by our table and looks my way. He doesn't say anything, but I can see it written all over his face. Milo knows he will win whatever battle we have going on. He tells me so by the slight curve of his lips and his raised brow.

I finally peel my eyes off Milo, stab a piece of steak, and bite into it. *She's right.*

This is the best steak I've ever had.

"Your family is fine with you hanging around him?" I ask, cutting another piece of steak. "I mean, I get who your brother is, but they're fine with you there all the time as well?"

"Well, my mother wasn't happy. My father thinks Morris is the best thing to ever happen to the family. And while I'm going to school—"

"You're in school?"

"Yep, to be a lawyer." She beams. "Part-time. I can't take it all on at once." She shakes her head and places her knife and fork down. "The club has helped me heaps. You know... they pay well too." She winks.

Dessert comes without us ordering it. I spot Milo in the corner, with a drink in hand, watching us. I flip him off, and he throws his head back and laughs before raising his glass to me. I try not to smile but fail miserably.

"You ready to head back?" Letti asks, pushing

away the plate from the brownie we just ate. "I'm so full."

"I can see why you come here. The food is great."

She nods in agreement. "Do you mind if we stop at my parents' house on the way home?" she asks.

"Should you be drinking?" Milo asks Letti, suddenly standing next to us.

"Should you be kissing women without their permission?" I ask in return. A few of his friends cough and laugh around us.

Letti excuses herself to chat with her brother. Even if she didn't have anything to say to Morris, I bet she would quickly find something to make herself scarce.

"I had permission. You're just slow to the party," he says matter-of-factly.

I raise a brow and step closer to him. "I never gave you permission. So does that mean I have permission to do as I please to you?"

"Yes, please." He smirks, and I have to stop the responding smile that wants to attach itself to my lips.

Stepping even closer so there is only a sliver of space between us, I lean up on my tippy-toes and get as close to his ear as possible. "You'll keep your lips to yourself, won't you?"

"Nope," he replies, and I reach between us and grip his cock, hard, through his jeans.

He stands there, unmoving, and stares at me. "I like it dirty. How dirty do you want to get, Pretty Lady? Can you handle it?"

"Keep your lips to yourself." I squeeze him briefly and then release before turning and striding straight out the door. I'm reaching for my cell when he walks out behind me.

"A kiss for a ride home," he offers.

I roll my eyes at him as Letti pokes her head around the door. "I'll be a bit, but if you don't want to hang around, Milo can take you. You have a key, right?" Her eyes dart to Milo, who nods before she looks back to me. I nod, too, not wanting to burden her any further.

"Get on the bike," he orders, putting the kickstand up and moving the bike so it's in front of me. Looking away, I take Letti's helmet he offers me and get on. This time, I don't need any help as I climb on behind him and wrap my arms around his waist. The air is cold on my hands, so I slip them into his jacket and under his shirt until I find his skin. He doesn't pull away or tell me to move my hands at the touch of my cool palms.

Leaning against him, he takes the turns slow and

steady, and if I didn't know any better, I would say he also took the long way home. When he gets to Letti's street, he slows down until we stop out front, where he turns off the bike and pulls his helmet off.

The first thing I smell as I take my own helmet off is his hair. I think that's where his rich leather scent comes from. Climbing off, I go to hand him the helmet, but he looks at it and back at me.

If those eyes could tell me a story, they would tell me how much he wants to devour me right now.

"Come back to the clubhouse with me?" he asks. I bite the inside of my cheek and shake my head. "Elizabeth." He reaches for my hand, but I pull it away before he can capture it.

I shouldn't form attachments while I'm still trying to repair myself.

That would be a stupid thing to do.

And I am far from stupid.

So why do I want to be stupid with him?

"I have to sleep. I'm tired." I walk up the path to the apartment, and when I get to the door, I look over my shoulder to see him still watching me. "Thanks for the lift, Milo."

I go inside before I change my mind.

Chapter 20

Milo

"Is watching someone for hours without moving considered creepy?"

She's been working for a week now, and while I let her work for the first few days without interruption, I just can't help myself by the end of the week.

"We all know why we're here," Axe says with a smirk.

"We come here all the fucking time," I remind him.

"Yes, we do, but not on a Friday." I ignore him as I watch Lissie come out from the back room. She doesn't know we're here as the bar is at the back, and our seats are situated at the front. Usually, we don't go up to the bar, but since I can't help myself, I stand and head that way.

Morris whistles from his seat at the table. "Oh, look at him go. He's in love."

I don't pay him any attention, as I leave them to do whatever the fuck it is they do. We have over twenty members in the Savage Villains, and while I respect each of them and think they all earned their spot here, it's those two dickheads I spend most of my time with.

As I get to the bar, I hear her say, "That will be twenty," to the patron she's serving. He hands her a fifty and tells her to keep the change. She beams and thanks him before her eyes find mine. Her smile drops, and a slow blush coats her cheeks. "Milo."

"Elizabeth." I lean on the bar so I'm closer to her.

I don't bother telling her that very soon, I will be killing her husband for non-payment. Instead, I focus on those killer eyes that suck me in every time I look into them.

And wonder when I can kiss her again.

Fuck, I want to kiss her.

"Would you tell Cody about us?" I ask her.

Her eyes shine with something I can't quite put a finger on before she answers, "How you like to kiss me, you mean?" she snarks.

"If I remember correctly, you kissed me back,

Pretty Lady." I wink at her, and she steps back far enough that I can appreciate her little black skirt and black tank top. She's also wearing boots, and her tattoos are on full display. I wonder if she has ink anywhere else. *Fuck, how I would like to know.* Her hair is back in a simple braid, a few strands framing her face.

"I guess you know you're a good kisser." She winks and walks over to the cash register. I watch as she puts the fifty in and then counts out her tip, putting it in her skirt pocket before she turns back to me. "Drunk people tip really well," she says, smiling.

"You know another way to earn a tip?" I sit my ass on the stool, and she stands in front of me on the other side of the bar.

"How?"

"Lean over, and I'll show you." I tap the bar, and her eyes flick to my hand before they come back to mine.

"I'm not kissing you again," she states, fighting a smirk.

"But I'll tip you."

"You know what tip I want? I want one where you have to pay me twenty thousand dollars." She huffs out a laugh and turns to start cleaning up the bar.

"Okay," I reply without hesitation.

She stops wiping down the bar and shoots me a disbelieving look. "Okay?"

"Okay. Twenty thousand, and I can kiss you right here, right now," I offer.

"Milo, are you all right?" she asks, moving closer. Despite the bar between us, I want to reach out and grab her. "Do you really have that sort of money to just throw around?"

"I do, and I can throw it where I fucking please. So, move a little closer."

"Just for a kiss?" she asks. "That's a life-changing amount of money for me." She shakes her head. "But I could never take it. I want to earn it."

"Oh, trust me, you'll be earning it. Those lips of yours are worth more than twenty grand." The lips in question pull up in a smile, and she shakes her head.

"Thanks for the job, Milo. I have to go back to work." She waves me off and goes to the other end of the bar.

And I sit there all night watching her.

Chapter 21

Lissie

"Shop till he drops me... in the bed, on the floor, or wherever. I'll take it."

"**P**retty Lady."

There's that voice again. The one that vibrates all the way through me without having permission to do so. I don't really understand my feelings for Milo. I'm not sure exactly what's happening between us, but it seems every warning I give myself to stay away isn't working. But how can I when any time I leave the house, he finds me? I get that it's a small town, but how unlucky—or lucky—am I?

I made a good amount in tips this week, and since I need so many things, I decided to go shopping. My hands clutch the new pair of shoes I was trying on as I close my eyes and take a deep breath. When I don't turn around to face Milo, he takes the seat next to me, pushing against me so our shoulders are touching.

"I prefer the black ones," he says, pointing to the heels on the stand in front of me.

"I have a cheaper pair already," I reply.

"I'd like to see you in them... just them and nothing else."

I huff out a breath and finally turn to face him. "Do you ever stop?" I ask.

"No, not when I want something as much as I want you."

"You should go find someone else. I'm sure it won't be that hard." I slide on the ballet flats I was holding.

"Are you saying I'm good-looking, Pretty Lady?" And I just know, without even seeing his face, he has a brow raised in amusement. When I turn slightly to check, I see I'm right.

"Those are ugly. You have long, beautiful legs. Get the heels." He stands, grabs the heels, and drops down in front of me on one knee. The shop lady watches with a mixture of amusement and horror on her face. I'm sure it's not every day men enter a ladies' shop dressed from head to toe in nothing but black leather, looking like he's there to kill someone.

He looks good, though.

Slipping the ballet flat from my foot, he slides the heel in its place. Then his hand works its way up my calf, stopping and gripping me just below my knee. His gaze traces all the way up my body until he reaches my eyes. The inspection is slow and sensual, and if I weren't a married woman, I would give in to what I know would be mind-blowing sex.

I'm sure Milo could provide very good mind-blowing sex.

"Get these heels."

"I told you, I have heels." I kick the shoe off.

"Let me get them and keep them at my place so when I fuck you after I finish reading the book to you, you can come while wearing these." I hear a lady gasp, but my eyes are glued to his, and I'm approaching the point where I don't care what anyone else thinks.

"I don't need you to buy me heels, Milo." I stand and tilt my head down to him. I slip on my own shoes when he doesn't move from his position.

"Oh, but you do," he says as he stands, towering over me. Then he leans in closer to smell me, getting in the crook of my neck but not quite touching me. "I'll be seeing you *real* soon." He pulls away, and as he leaves, his sandalwood scent surrounds me. I wonder when I'll start hating that smell.

Probably never.

* * *

"So I'm not sure how interested you may be, but there is a party tonight at the clubhouse," Letti says, coming out of her room in a short silk dress.

"You look beautiful," I tell her.

She gives me a small spin and then a curtsy. "Why, thank you, my lady, but I got you one too."

I look at her, surprised. I've been paying her money now, even if it's hard to get her to accept it. I want to chip in and help as much as I can.

She goes back into her room and then comes back out, holding a bag. "Take it. There was a buy-one, get-one-half-price sale, and I couldn't resist it."

I take the bag from her and pull out a little black dress with spaghetti straps and a small slit up the side.

"Please say you'll come with me. Obviously, there's no pressure, but I'd love for you to come with me."

I glance down at the dress and then raise my eyes back to her. "I will, if that's okay." I hold up the dress. "And thank you so much for this. It's beautiful." I turn and head to my bedroom. I slip into the dress and leave my Docs on my feet. When I come back out, she has her keys and is ready to go.

When we arrive at the clubhouse, I don't see him right away. I sit with Aiden at the fire as he tells stories while Letti goes to the bar and takes shots with Mason. By the fifth shot, I think I should go over and help her, but I stay where I am, not wanting to be *that* friend.

"You loving your new job?" Aiden asks.

"I am, it's good. I earn good money, too," I say, smiling as he hands me a drink. I take a small sip. I used to drink a lot when I first met Cody, but ever since I stopped, I just don't feel the need to do it again. Maybe it's because I didn't want my inhibitions lowered around him. Some part of me stopped trusting him somewhere along the way.

"I'm so happy you came. So, so happy." Letti's arms wrap around me from behind as she slurs in my ear.

"You're drunk," I state.

She rolls her eyes and waves me off. "Almost. And, gosh, it feels good." Just then, Mason walks over, and she pulls him to her and leans on his chest. "This is Mason. He's who I've been fucking."

"I know who Mason is," I tell her, smirking at

Mason. "I would ask how the fucking is going, but I don't really want to know."

Letti laughs. "Oh, it's good. Best I've ever had." She taps his chest. "Isn't that right, Mason?"

He peers down at her, holding her hip. "If you say so." He looks back at me. "Milo, know you're here?"

"Nope."

"I'll let him know."

"Don't. I'm not here for him."

He raises a brow. "You aren't?"

"Nope. I came with Letti to celebrate," I reply.

"Hello, Pretty Lady." A hand slides around my waist, and Mason turns, taking Letti with him as she giggles and waves at me. I pull out of Milo's grip and turn around to face him.

"Want to get out of here?" he asks, leaning in too close for comfort. I step away without replying and move in the direction of where everyone is gathered. A few people look my way, and as I go to sit in an open seat, someone growls.

"Move." And the man next to me gets up without hesitation, and now Milo is situated right next to me. "Are you drinking, Pretty Lady?"

"Why do you call her that?" Letti asks, interrupting us.

"Because that's what she is, even if she's never realized it," Milo explains. He turns to me. "I have your book."

"You are a book thief! You know that, right?"

Everyone around us chuckles.

"I only steal yours," he replies.

Letti grabs another drink, and I hold out my hand. She passes it to me before she sits back down next to Mason. People talk, and music blares, and all the while, Milo stays seated next to me.

"You're drinking. Is that a wise decision?" he asks.

"Who do you plan to annoy when I'm no longer here?" I ask, taking a sip.

"You're leaving?" he says, surprised.

"Of course I am. What's keeping me in this place apart from my current lack of money?"

"I didn't think it would be so soon."

"Yep. Once I get enough, I'm gone."

Letti gets up and starts dancing with some guy, and Mason watches her with dark eyes. A few people join in, and I look to Milo. "What do you want from me, Milo?"

He leans in close. "Just you. Give me you, just for tonight."

His words eat at me. My gaze flicks to his lips

and then back to his eyes. *What would it mean to give myself to him, even for a night?*

"A one-night stand?" I whisper.

"If you want to call it that."

"One night?"

"It's all it will take." His lips are basically on mine now, and I pull back and stare into his eyes.

"Where?" I ask.

He doesn't waste any time as he stands, strides over to Morris, leans down to say something in his ear, then pats him on the back before he comes back to me. He takes my hand, pulls me up, and leads us straight to his bike. Putting my helmet on my head, he climbs on, and I follow.

Glancing back over my shoulder, I see Letti watching me, and I give her a wave before we take off into the unknown.

Chapter 22

Milo

"Perfection in a silk dress."

I gave her husband one extra week.

He begged and begged.

I didn't do it for him, though.

I did it for her.

He doesn't need to know that, though.

She sits behind me in that little black dress and her combat boots, and I have to remind myself that she was not made for me, no matter how much I want it to be otherwise.

She plans to leave, and I would never ask her to stay for the simple fact that she is more than this place. This place is nothing compared to who she could be.

Elizabeth is utter perfection. Currently wrapped in a silk dress and pressed up against me.

I don't know how to describe it, but she makes me lose all sense of myself, and I want to do everything in my power to put a smile on her face.

Hell, I was ready to pay her twenty thousand dollars just to get those lips touching mine.

I would have paid her more.

I would have given her anything she asked for.

I'd always watched her from afar, and when the opportunity came up to have pieces of her that her stupid fucking husband was so willing to give away, I took it.

At first, I had no idea what I planned to make her do, but as she sat there quietly, I grabbed a book and asked her to read it. As time went on, I bought more, just so she could read them to me.

I would buy every book in this fucking city if I could get her to read them to me. Fuck, the way she sounds when she reads some of the scenes, the way her voice turns breathy...

I get why women read.

I get it so fucking much.

My perfect little bookworm, who is about to make me one fucking happy man tonight.

I hope.

Chapter 23

Lissie

"Is it a one-night stand?"

Sex. Is that what I expect from Milo? Absolutely.

But I assumed we would have it in his room at the clubhouse. Instead, he drives through town and farther out. I don't ask him where he's taking me because I know I'm safe with him. And although some would probably think me deranged for going away with a ruthless killer, I don't care. Everyone knows he's as ruthless as he looks, and if he wanted me dead, I would have been by now.

Nerves start to hit me when he turns down a gravel driveway and slows his bike. With only a few lights on up ahead to guide us, he drives up to a large white fence, hops off the bike, and pushes the gate open. What's on the other side of it is what looks like a massive country home. It's a two- possibly three-story white barn-style house with a blue roof. Lush green landscaping and a few garden beds cover the grounds around the house. He maneuvers down the white gravel and comes to a stop out front. The porch light shines on us as he turns off his bike. I climb off and remove my helmet, and when I turn to him, he's standing next to me and studying my reaction.

"Where are we?" I ask.

He glances at the house and back to me. "My house," he states.

I'm in awe. Really, I am. This place is a dream from the outside—well-maintained and doesn't look like it's owned by a bad-ass biker.

"Since when?"

"I started building it when I was seventeen. I found the land, and my father bought it for me. It took me over five years." He grabs my hand and pulls me in the direction of the house, and I go with him willingly. He puts his thumb on a scanner next to the door, and it unlocks, letting us in.

"So if I just cut off your thumb, I'd have access as well?" I joke.

He stops inside, pushes a few buttons, then reaches for my hand again and presses my finger on the pad for a few moments. When the scan is done, he drops my hand.

"Now you can enter whenever you please."

"What if I rob you?"

"Rob me blind, Pretty Lady. It would only give me an excuse to track you down."

I turn away from him—his words making my girl parts flutter—and take in the interior of the house. Wooden floors stretch from wall to wall, their rich grain adding warmth to the space. The living room features brown leather couches adorned with colorful throw cushions. The space opens to a kitchen, which is also decorated in warm brown tones. Accent rugs provide a pop of color to break up the brown color palette.

Upstairs, an elegant iron railing encircles the open landing, giving a sense of openness. Strategically placed lights shine and cast a soft glow that highlights every corner.

"This place is beautiful," I say, wandering farther in and not thinking too much about the fact that he just gave me full permission to come and go as I please. "Is it just you who lives here?"

"Yes, I prefer it that way."

"But you stay a lot at the clubhouse?"

"Yes. But if I had a choice, it would be here."

"How can you afford this?" This place has to be worth a lot, with its high-end finishes, spacious layout, and attention to detail. The quality craftsmanship shines through in every room.

"I can afford a lot of things," he muses, kicking off his boots. "You'll spend the night. As you said, though, only one night."

"One-night stand usually means the other leaves after it's done."

"You have a lot of one-night stands?" he asks, anger in his tone.

"No, I never really thought about it."

"You will stay the whole night. And in the morning, I'll take you back. Until then, get naked."

I gape at him. "You get naked," I bite back.

He shrugs as if it's nothing and instantly starts pulling off his vest, placing it on the back of the couch next to where I'm standing, then reaches for his shirt. Crossing his hands at the hem, he pulls it over his head and off. If eyes could drool, mine would be right now.

Toned.

Muscular.

Tattooed.

His tattoos don't form any sort of pattern. They

look randomly placed as if on a canvas where the artist has gone mad. But it works.

Milo unbuckles his belt and tugs it through the loops, then drops it to the floor. He unbuttons his jeans without looking up or even caring that I'm ogling him. I stare as he pulls them down, leaving him in only boxers. Then, without a second thought, he removes those as well.

Standing before me is a man.

And I mean... *a man.*

Cock hard and long, a neatly shaved patch of hair surrounding the base, as if he keeps himself manicured, though he doesn't give the impression that he does. Would I have thought of his cock as manicured before? Probably not, but now I know with absolute certainty I will.

"Elizabeth." My eyes jump from his cock to meet his heated gaze. "You have drool... here." He taps the corner of his lips. "Now, strip."

I suck in a breath, then remind him, "I have scars."

"I couldn't care less. Remove it all."

I take a deep breath before I do as he says. I mean, he is naked, too, after all. Reaching for the hem of my black silk dress, I slip it off easily. His eyes trace my body, and I pause to watch him. His gaze roams over my red lace bra and then drops to my stomach, and I resist the urge to cover it. I have small scars from falls I don't remember and burns from being too fucked-up.

"Matching lingerie. Were you planning on fucking someone tonight?"

"My underwear always matches," I inform him. He says something under his breath as I reach behind me and unclip my bra. As it slips down my arms, he steps forward and takes it from my hand, leaving me standing in front of him in only my red lace panties.

This is so weird. I've been with one man, and never did he look at me the way Milo is staring at me right now—as if he's ready to devour me, and I am more than happy to let him. If only to see what it would be like to have someone want you that badly.

"We need to be careful we don't hurt you," he says, keeping my bra in his grasp, then circles his arms around me, lifting me up so my legs wrap around his waist, then takes me to the stairs and up them as if I weigh nothing. We come to another large, open area, but this one has a huge fireplace with a bed in front of it. There are big bay windows with gorgeous blue curtains. His bedding is brown with white sheets.

He gently lays me down on the soft mattress, and I realize he also brought my clothes up with him, which are now on the floor dropped at his feet.

"Elizabeth."

"Hmm?" I hum as he pulls away. Milo leans over to a bedside table and grabs a condom, and I put my hand up to stop him.

"You can put it on," he says.

"I want you to crawl to me," I state. Moving to the end of the bed, I open my legs and lean forward, my breasts swaying gently.

"Shouldn't I be saying that?" he asks.

"If you want to play, you play, but I want to be in charge." I smirk, feeling more wanted and desired than ever before. I've never been with someone like Milo. Someone who holds so much power out of the bedroom that I want to see how far he'll allow me to go. I want to test it, and as I watch him drop to his knees, I grin.

I wonder what else I can get him to do. Now, that is an interesting thought.

"I would make you crawl, but we can't scare you... yet." He moves toward me. He doesn't crawl, though. He prowls like a deadly assassin, closing in on their kill.

And I am that kill.

When he reaches me, he shuffles between my legs and goes to crawl on top of me, but I stop him with a finger to his mouth. He licks my finger, and I smile.

"Where do you think you're going?" I ask. "Lie on your back and pass me the condom." He does so without argument, stretching out on the bed. I stand and hook my fingers into my panties, sliding them off and leaving them at my feet. Then I move over to him and place a foot on either side of him. His hands go behind his head, and he watches me with amusement.

"I'm resisting the urge," he says.

"What urge?"

"To throw you around like a rag doll, Pretty Lady. But because I want you to know this night is all about you, I won't."

"You're talking like I don't always have full control, Mr. Savage." I wink and lower myself to his thighs, just behind his cock. It twitches as I settle in. Ripping the condom wrapper, I open it and study his cock.

"It sure is a pretty cock." I smile, and just as he thinks I'm about to slide the condom on him, I grip his cock, lower my head, and wrap my lips over the tip. He pulls his hands from behind his head, and I instantly stop. Wiping my mouth, I grin at him. "Put your hands back where they were," I tell him, and he does so with eager eyes.

When Cody and I used to sleep together, I would try to take control, and he hated it and told me that's not a woman's job. Our sex life was dull and boring.

Leaning forward, I kiss the tip, my tongue swirling around the head before I take him all in my mouth. With my hand that's not holding the condom, I stroke the shaft up and down, and his hips move with each stroke.

"As much as I love this, stop." I do as he says and pull back. Sliding the condom onto his hard cock, I shuffle my hips forward until I'm basically riding him without him being inside me.

"Can I move my hands now?" he asks. I lean forward, making sure my clit is rubbing against him, and start moving. I've found by using a vibrator that my favorite way to be stimulated is from the outside, with plenty of pressure. I never once came with Cody—it was all about him. I had to learn on my own what I like and how to make myself come.

And that's what I did.

I touch my lips to his as I circle my hips. Milo moves his hands and threads them through my hair, pulling it free from its bun so it falls in my face, but that doesn't stop our kiss.

I'm not sure anything would stop us at this point. He thrusts up to meet me as I grind on him, and then he slides a hand between us and slips himself inside me. I gasp into his mouth, but he holds me to him, gripping my ass and sliding me up and down.

So I can feel every movement.

Every. Single. One.

The pressure on my clit, the fullness, and something inside make me feel like I just need to keep moving my hips. He gets it and takes full control, all the while not breaking our kiss.

He has skills.

And he knows exactly what he's doing, and he's doing it well.

My hands tangle in his hair, and he's careful not to hurt me, his touch and his movements tender, but I know he's holding back.

I wonder what it would be like to fuck him with no obstacles because what he is doing right now is so simple, yet it's the most pleasure I have ever felt.

I can't think like that, though.

One night, and that's it.

Gripping his hair, I feel myself starting to come.

"Don't you fucking dare!" He stops thrusting, his

hands on my ass, halting my movements. I try to fight against him, but all he does is smirk. "I let you have your playtime, Pretty Lady. Now it's my turn." He sits up carefully, still inside me, but as I go to lift off him, he shakes his head. I listen, not really sure why, as he flips us so he's on top. He pulls out, but as he does, he mutters a swear word.

"What's wrong?" I ask, going to cover up, but he moves my hand away.

"Where did you go just then, in your head?" he asks. Standing, he walks to the closet and gets something, and then he stops at the bed to grab two pillows before returning to me.

When I don't answer, his eyes lock on me. "Elizabeth. Where did you just go in your head?" I say nothing. "Never cover up around me." His voice drops to a low growl, and he leans down, his cock still hard.

He lifts my head gently and places a pillow under it. "You'll tell me if I get too rough?" he asks, his hand caressing down my neck, fingers dragging between my breasts before they stop on my stomach. "Lift." I'm confused at first until he taps my hips. "Lift." I do, and he slides the other pillow under my lower back and buttocks. "Are you okay?" Milo questions before he reaches for whatever he brought from the closet.

"It's all new, never been used," he assures me as he pulls out a cock ring. I've seen them but never used one. Then he opens the second box. Two little clamps sit inside. I scrunch my brows before he smiles. "For you."

"Will it hurt?" I ask.

"Only in the best possible way."

And I believe him.

Chapter 24

Lissie

"How long can a one-night stand actually last?"

I'm having a one-night stand with the town's bad boy.

I never thought that sentence would refer to me and Milo, but I'm really glad it does.

Milo Savage has been a torment for me for years. He's filtered his way into my thoughts without permission. I've tried not to give it too much thought, but it's hard when it comes to this man.

"Where did you go?"

I glance at Milo, those dark eyes staring back at me.

"I was thinking about you," I confess.

"And?"

"Have you ever been in love, Milo?"

His brows raise at the question. "You want to talk

about love while I'm about to fuck you?" He chuckles. "Maybe another day. I only have one night, right?" His last words are absolutely a question—he wants to know if he'll truly only get one night with me.

"You know that's how it has to be."

"If you say so." He doesn't sound convinced as he slides on the cock ring and then moves toward me. Pushing my legs to either side, he situates himself on his knees between them. Leaning forward, he takes my nipple into his mouth. He tastes, his tongue swirling around the bud before he bites it ever so lightly. I go to thread my fingers through his hair, and he stops what he's doing, lifts his head from my puckered nipple, and places a clamp on it. I peer down—the pressure is a lot, but it's nice. I like it. *How did I not know they would feel this good?* When he applies the clamp on the other nipple, I breathe a heavy sigh of relief that they are both the same now.

He sits back on his heels and pushes my legs farther apart. His fingertips stroke up and down my stomach, teasing me as he gets closer and closer to where I need him. He can tell I want him to go lower because each time he does, I lift my hips to show him, and soft moans leave my mouth in anticipation of what's about to come.

Us.

And the desperation is getting real now.

His feather-light touches continue their journey down my body until they're on my pussy, where he strokes me back and forth before he slips a finger between my folds and smirks. "So wet. What a good girl you are." And he slides a finger inside me. "Oh, what a *very* good girl you are." He hums. "Your pussy wants more, doesn't it?" I nod rapidly as my fingers tangle in the sheets by my hips. "Such a tight cunt." He pulls his finger out and drops down, his mouth now the one doing the teasing. He kisses my pussy, then sticks his tongue out and slides it up and down. I groan, and he chuckles against me as he reaches up to tighten the clamps with one hand while his mouth blows hot air on me.

I'm getting impatient now.

I just need... *him.*

And all he wants to do is play. Not that I don't appreciate the teasing, but it's not what my body is screaming for. Maybe that's his trick, though. To tease me until I break, and all my thoughts are of him and how fast he can fill me.

That's his plan—I just know it.

"Milo."

"Hmm?"

"You won't win this game." But I know it's a lie as it slips from my lips. He chuckles as he moves up to my nipple, licking it again and breathing hot air over it as his devilish eyes lock on mine.

"I've been losing games with you for as long as I can remember, Pretty Lady. You just never realized I was playing." He pulls back, and his gaze skates over me, taking me all in.

From my scars to my breasts to my bare pussy.

"Milo."

"Hmm?" He touches my inner thigh, stroking it softly before sliding up farther to touch me between my legs.

"I don't want to play games anymore. I want to be fucked." His brows hitch up as his eyes dance with mischief, and his hot stare penetrates me. He raises off me and stands, and my body feels cold without him. I go to get up, but the look he gives me stops me in my place.

"Did I say you can move?" he asks, and I bite my lip. A knock sounds at the door, but both of us ignore it.

My gaze tracks him as he goes to the closet again, and before I can move, he's back, with a smirk on his face and the heels he made me try on the other day dangling from his fingers. "Put them on."

"I told you I already have heels."

"And I told you... I would keep a pair here to fuck you in," he explains.

"So confident that you would fuck me?" I chuckle, and he taps my leg. When I don't move quickly enough for him, he grabs my foot and slides the black heel on it, then does the same on the other foot. Sinister eyes lock on me as if I am his prey.

"Get on all fours," he growls, frustrated, before he sits down on the bed and studies me with those chocolate eyes.

One would think being naked in front of a man like him would be intimidating. But it makes me feel powerful, knowing someone like him wants me. I do as he says and turn around, pushing the pillow away as I get on all fours. "Turn," he commands, and I obey.

"Stop." I do, with my ass facing him, and I hear the bed creak as another knock comes from downstairs.

"Fucking hell," he mutters before I feel heat at my entrance. His mouth is there, and his tongue slides in, making me jump. He chuckles and places a hand on my back to keep me from moving. His tongue finds spots down there I didn't even know existed. Each lick and suck is like a whole new experience until he pulls away. And before I can process what's happening, he slides into me so painfully slow that I try to push back on him. But he knows how greedy I am already and grips my hips with his strong hands, holding me in place.

"Lissie." My name is called, and I know it's Letti. I pause, but Milo couldn't care less about the possible intrusion. He thrusts, and I have to remember not to scream.

Fuck.

It feels good.

He slides in and out, one hand reaching around me to find my clit. He plays with me as his cock pistons in and out, and it feels like heaven.

It isn't long before my hands are forming fists, and my back is arching to try to slow the wave of pleasure that is about to hit me full force.

He keeps a perfect pace, fucking me as if he knows exactly what spots to hit and how to please me.

If I were a woman who fell in love because of a cock, I would be in love with this man in a heartbeat. Or so I keep telling myself.

When I come, he slaps my ass as he removes his fingers from my clit, then he takes hold of my hips and pushes in as deep as he can.

I groan, and my body starts to fall forward, but he catches me with his arm around my stomach, not once slowing his movements.

"Pretty Lady," he growls. I push back on him, and he chuckles before I feel him come, too. He grunts, says my name, and slaps my ass again before he pulls out. And just before I can collapse, he manages to slide one of the pillows under me. I hear him take a few steps before the rustle of clothes hits my ears.

Another knock sounds louder this time, and he walks out of the room. I hear voices, so I kick the heels off before grabbing whatever clothes I can find and slipping them on. Then I go to see what Letti wants.

"I'll bring her back after we sleep," I hear Milo say.

"Sleep?" Letti's voice echoes down the hall.

"Prez—" I hear Mason start.

"You are guests in my house, and she—"

"She what?" I interrupt, stopping at the top of the stairs.

All eyes fall on me.

"Get back in the bedroom," Milo growls, looking up at me. He smacks Mason on the back of the head, making him turn his face away.

"Cody came around," Letti says.

My brows scrunch together. "Just now?" I ask.

She bites her lip. "It was earlier. It's why I wanted you to come to the clubhouse so badly."

"You didn't want to tell me?" I say in surprise. I had all my calls redirected to her phone in case my sister called since I didn't have my phone.

"I wanted you to have fun, but Mason insisted I tell you."

Mason nods his head.

"You need to divorce him," Mason adds. "You'll need a good lawyer."

I feel sick at his words.

"Do you want to come home?" Letti asks. "I feel bad being here. I mean, you and Milo..." she trails off.

"What did Cody want?" I inquire tiredly.

"He asked to see you," she whispers. "I lied..."

"I'll come back with you. Let me get my things."

I run back into the bedroom to collect my things without sparing Milo a glance. Not even a minute later, he's there, holding my jacket in his hand, which I slip on. I take a moment to appreciate his body, as this is the only time I'll see him this way. He's all toned muscles, and ink trails down his chest to that perfect V where his jeans hang low.

"Goodbye, Pretty Lady," he says, leaning against the wall.

My eyes find his chocolate ones, and I suck in a breath.

He is beautiful.

In every single way possible.

Cody was pretty, in that boy-next-door, eat-your-heart-out kind of way, but that changed. Milo is drop-your-panties-and-call-him-Daddy sexy. He gets better with age.

I go to speak, but words don't come out, so I give him a soft smile before I step past him and out the door.

Letti stares at me but remains silent.

What is there to say? I was having the best sex of my life, and she and Mason came and ruined it.

But the truth is...

Reality was always waiting.

Chapter 25

Milo

"To kill or not to kill, that is the question."

I tried; I really did.

Telling myself that one night would be enough, but I was lying to myself as much as I was lying to her. And the fact that she may be leaving, fucking sucks more than it should.

"I gave you access to my home because I trust you, and you just stepped right the fuck in without any warning," I say to Mason. He chews his bottom lip nervously.

"Letti was upset. I don't fucking want her upset. I made a rash decision, and I'm sorry," he says, shaking his head. "I'm sorry, Prez."

"Get the fuck out of my house," I grit out, pointing toward the door.

He nods and leaves.

I head back into the bedroom, where I picture Lissie's beautiful fucking body everywhere. The way she moans, the way the moans slip from her lips.

She was in control—I let her have it—and I wonder if that fucking piece of shit husband ever gave that to her.

I can answer...

Categorically, he did not!

Chapter 26

Lissie

"Divorce is the only way."

As I have consecutive days working at the bar, I don't see Milo for the rest of the week. My job brings in good money, and that makes me happy. Mason has also set me up with a lawyer so I can get the divorce settled. I sent Cody the papers in the middle of the week, and to be honest, I just hoped it would be nice and straightforward, and he would sign them without any hassle, but I think that's expecting too much from a man who always gave me so little.

"That man over there has been asking for you. Do you want me to send him off?" Chastity says, motioning her thumb over her shoulder. I look past her and see Cody staring at me from the other end of the bar. His eyes are locked on mine, and he is *not* happy. In his hand is a stack of papers.

"No, it's okay. Can you cover for me?"

She turns back and eyes Cody. "Should I call anyone? He doesn't look friendly," she asks in concern. I think about her question, but I really don't want to bring attention to myself. I like this job, and while I plan to leave the city when I have enough money, I want to stay here as long as possible to earn as much as I can.

"No, just maybe check on me in ten?"

She nods, and I brush my hands down my apron as I step out from behind the bar. I come face-to-face with Cody, and he looks like shit, worse than before.

"Hi," I say, then glance at the papers. "I see you got my mail."

"Yeah, about that. I'm *not* signing."

"Why? We aren't together, Cody." I lean in and hiss, "You tied me to the fucking bed, and what? You expected me to just skip on home?" He bites the inside of his cheek as his mouth forms a straight line. "It's been weeks since I left you," I remind him.

"And you're already fucking someone else," he sneers. I tense at his words. He holds up the papers. "Come home, and stop this shit." He throws the papers at my feet, and I bend to pick them up.

I look up at him and shake my head. "I'm never coming back to you. That was a sad part of my life, and I can see that it's not where I want to be." Before I can say anything more, he slaps me across the face. I fall back, my ass hitting the floor. Just as I try to get up, someone grabs hold of Cody, stopping him from hitting me again.

"I suggest you walk out before I drag you out," Milo says, voice low and menacing, his eyes darker than I have ever seen them as he grips Cody's wrist, turning his hand pink. Cody nods and glares down at me. He doesn't say anything, but the narrowing of his eyes tells me he is furious. As he turns to leave, I'm lifted from the floor and smashed into the front of Milo as he holds me. "Are you okay?" he asks. He doesn't ease his hold on me while he waits for me to answer.

"Yes, I'm fine. Thanks for that."

Milo nods but keeps his grip on me. "I've missed you," he whispers, and I instantly feel guilty. I have been beating myself up all week. I slept with a man who is not my husband. And I really fucking enjoyed it. Raising my head, I smile up at him.

"Thank you again," I say, ignoring what he said.

"Come over after work... to get your book."

"I can't, I have plans."

"I'll come for you in two nights, then."

"Okay," I reply, unable to say no. "You can let me go now." I lift a brow at him.

He lays a hand on my face and brushes it against my cheek, where I know it's red from Cody's slap.

"I'll punish him for this," he growls.

"Don't kill him," I whisper, and he eyes me with a smirk.

"If I don't kill him, what do I get in return?"

"If you don't kill him, I'll come get my book. But if he's dead, I won't."

"Done," he says and releases me, turning to leave. *Shit, I didn't say* not *to hurt him.* I chase after Milo and out the door. The minute I step out and the cold air hits my skin, I watch as Milo, strong and powerful, walks straight up to Cody, who is being held in place by Axe, and he throws his fist into Cody's stomach. I gasp loudly, and Milo turns around to face me.

"You didn't mention I couldn't hurt him." He winks and then turns back and punches Cody again.

I stand there, shocked.

I mean, I really shouldn't be, considering who Milo is.

But I watch as his fists pummel into my husband

with malice and without an ounce of remorse. In fact, he wears a smirk on his lips.

"Stop!" I yell, and Milo's fists do, in fact, stop. Then he steps back and turns to me.

"This is who you associate with now?" Cody says with ragged, hard breaths. Axe lets go of him, and he falls to the ground like a piece of shit. His hands land on the gravel, and his gaze falls away from me.

I look to Milo, who is now standing in front of me.

"Let him go."

"I can't do that." He shakes his head. "I already agreed not to kill him."

"You made him agree not to kill me?" Cody shouts.

"She saved your fucking life," Milo says, then turns and stalks over to Cody. "Now, apologize for talking to her that way."

"I should have tied you to that bed long before I did," Cody growls at me, but it's Milo whose lips start to twitch as he rolls up the sleeves of his long black shirt and steps closer to Cody.

"You *tied her to the bed*?" Milo grits through his teeth.

"Yeah, and the bitch escaped."

I wince, and Milo's gaze flings back to me and

moves to my wrists, where I've been rubbing them without realizing it. Before I do anything to stop him, he turns back around and kicks Cody so hard I hear a loud snap. Cody falls back to the ground in a heap.

"Oh my God, what did you do?" I screech, my hands covering my face.

"Go back inside, Elizabeth." A shiver runs down my spine at the tone in Milo's voice.

"You won't kill him?" I ask, stepping toward them.

Milo blocks my path. "Not right now, no." He takes a deep breath, then asks. "You escaped, right? That's why your wrists were red?"

I look down at my wrists, which are fully healed, and nod.

"You really don't want me to kill him? I could and would... for you." His tone softens, and I look into those beautiful eyes, the very same ones that can be harsh and cold to everyone else.

"No, please don't." I shake my head.

Milo reaches up, brushes his thumb over my cheek again, then nods. "Okay. Go inside, please."

I nod like a zombie and turn to head back inside. Not once do I look back to see what they do with Cody. Milo said he wouldn't kill him, so that's as much as I can hope for now.

"You okay?" Chastity asks as I round the bar.

"Yes."

"Are you sure? I can cover for you if you need a little more time."

I look around at the patrons waiting to be served. "No, it's fine." I take a cleansing breath and go back to work.

I didn't realize sending Cody divorce papers would come to this. To be honest, I had hoped he would just let it all go.

Let *me* go.

Clearly, I am never going back to him, no matter what. I'm trying to put that part of my life behind me and move on. I can't do that still being attached to Cody—legally, that is. Physically and mentally, we haven't been together in two years.

Not only have I concluded that my life with Cody will never work, but Milo has also made me realize that I like to be desired and wanted by someone. I guess I never really had that with Cody. Not that, at the beginning, we did have a sex life, but even then, it was nothing that I'd tell my friends about.

And then, along the way, that stopped as well. I don't think he loved me. I'm bewildered as to why Cody's fighting this so hard. We both moved on while we were still together. I used to find him all the time, touching himself, and not once did he ask me to join him.

And then there was the matter of *all* the women. I get that he made his money by basically pimping them out. And he made it very clear that I had to be thankful that these women were willing to spread their legs to put food on our table.

That's when I *really* knew he didn't love me.

But I stayed like a lovesick fool trapped in an environment I didn't know how to escape. You read about how women stay in bad relationships and wonder why. But when it happens to you, you don't always realize it until it's too late.

I had no one.

He isolated me.

And I let him.

I drifted away from any friends I had growing up until I only had him.

During that time, my sister was nowhere to be found. She was drugged up herself, so it was just Cody.

Despite how much I don't love him and how poorly he treated me, I don't want Cody dead, and I think Milo is a man of his word.

At least, I hope he is.

Chapter 27

Milo

"She should have always been mine."

When the door shuts behind her, I crouch down to look at the piece of shit lying in the gravel at my feet. It's dark, and the only illumination we have is from the light over the bar's entrance door, but it's enough for me to see Cody's face is red, and he's knocked out cold.

"Take him out back," I tell Axe.

I open an app on my phone to turn off the cameras at the back of the bar as he lifts Cody and carries him into the darkness, where no one can see us.

"Fuck, he's heavy." Axe grunts when he drops Cody to the ground, and Cody starts to wake up.

We stand there and wait.

Cody's hands start to twitch in the dirt, and his eyes slowly open. When he's fully awake, he lifts his hand and winces. "What—"

"You think it's fun to hurt your wife?" I ask.

Axe hands me his knife, and I grip it tightly in my hand.

Cody looks up and tries to scramble backward, but he doesn't get far. "She is *my* wife, not yours. You've been jealous of that fact for years," he spits. He sounds angry, but his face tells me another story. He's scared. Petrified. "If you kill me, she'll hate you."

"Oh, Prez, he thinks he can talk his way out of what's about to happen to him." Axe laughs.

Cody's worried gaze slides to Axe before coming back to me.

"You see, Cody, I've been very lenient with you, and you have abused that generosity. The last man who thought he could get away with abusing my *somewhat* better nature ended up in the fucking morgue with no one to identify him because he was already ashes." I smile at him. "Now, tell me again why I can't kill you?"

"You told her you won't," he says desperately.

"But I didn't say I wouldn't hurt you." I nod to Axe, who moves behind Cody, locking his arm around Cody's neck so he can't move. Cody's hands go straight to Axe's arm, and he tries to pull free, but Axe has a strong-ass fucking grip, and no one can get out of his hold.

I bend down and smile.

"Not only are you scum, not only do you owe me, and I have let you live, but you also fucked with the wrong person." I reach for his hand, which is trying desperately to pull Axe's arm from around his neck, but with no luck, I pull it toward me. He tries his hardest to tug it back, but I smile at him as I push it to the ground and then step on it to keep it there.

"Please, don't. I'll get the money... I-I just need more time," he whines with his eyes locked on his hand under my boot.

"Time is something I have already given you plenty of, Cody. My time is precious, and you are wasting it. But that's not what this is about. After this, no one else will be able to save you. Not even *her*." I hold the knife above his hand, and he tries to scrunch his fingers up. "Place all five fingers on the ground, *now*," I warn him.

"No, please," he begs.

"*Now*."

"No," he says again, and I slam the blade

straight down into his hand. The knife shifts through the flesh, and his screams rip through the night.

"Open your hand, now." He does so, but tears are rolling down his face, and Axe holds him tighter as he struggles. I pull the knife out, and his cries become louder. His hand is bleeding as he splays his fingers flat on the ground. "Good. Now start fucking listening," I tell him.

He continues to cry as I bend down. He watches the knife in my hand with watery eyes as I put it closer to his hand again. I know he wants to pull his hand away, but now he knows what will happen if he does so again. "See, you *can* listen," I say as I bring the knife down and chop off the tip of his pinkie finger. He screams, and as Cody passes out, Axe holds him tighter.

"He stinks," Axe grumbles, letting him go.

I take out a tissue, pick up the tip of his finger, and wrap it up before standing. Handing it to Axe, who takes it before we look down at Cody.

"She really married him?" he asks. "She can *for sure* do better." He winks at me.

I shake my head at him before we walk back to the front. As we get to our bikes, Elizabeth comes out, her hands wrapped around her midsection, and she looks around. Axe starts his bike and waits for me as I sit on mine.

"Has Cody left?" she asks.

"Kind of," I tell her.

"Thanks for not... you know." She shrugs.

"I'll take payment now if you don't mind."

"I told you, I have plans tonight." Her arms drop from around her waist.

"No, I'm not talking about *that* payment." I reach for her and pull her closer. Grabbing her with both hands, I lift her and put her between my legs on the bike. She has to straddle me, and I look down to where her skirt rides up and see red panties.

"Milo."

"Hmm?"

"My face is up here." She places a finger under my chin and lifts it.

"But the lips I want to kiss are down here." I move my hand from her waist and slide it between her legs. Her eyes track the movement before she stops me with her hand.

"Thank you for listening," she says.

"I'll always listen to you." Something flashes in her eyes, and she leans in, presses her lips to mine, and quickly pulls back.

"Help me off. I have to finish my shift," Lissie

says, and I do as she asks, lifting her back up. She leans forward with her hands on my shoulders as I place her back on her feet.

"Milo," she says, stepping away from my grasp.

"Yes, Elizabeth?" I smile at her.

"I look forward to using that bike for more than riding." She winks and turns, running back toward the bar.

Axe starts laughing. "You're in trouble" is the only thing he says as I start my bike, and I don't bother agreeing with him.

Because I was in trouble the moment I first fucking saw her.

Chapter 28

Lissie

"Drunk dial?"

I don't tell Letti about Cody showing up at the bar.

I figure it's not her problem.

She's already been the best friend I could ever have hoped for.

I bought a new phone last week, and she is the only person with the number, besides work and my lawyer. I prefer it that way.

"It's your birthday tomorrow," Letti mentions as she hands me another black dress.

"You already got me a dress, remember?" She smiles and claps her hands. "I know, but my love language is giving gifts, so if you tell me you don't want it, it will hurt my feelings." I see a twinkle in her eyes as she says it.

"Are you sure your love language isn't bribery?" I throw back, laughing as I examine the dress.

"When was the last time you went out for a girls' night and simply had fun?" she asks. I stare down at the dress and go quiet. "There's this club in town that serves mean cocktails, and I plan to try every one of them." She goes on, asking while peering down at her shoes, "What's your favorite cocktail?" She's wearing a tiny pink dress and black heels. Honestly, she looks so stinking cute with her blonde hair in curls and her perfect smile.

"I haven't ever really had a cocktail... or a girls' night," I finally say.

Her head jerks up, eyes going wide. "What? Okay, well, that works out perfectly. You and I are celebrating. No men allowed." She nods as if that's an order. "Now, go and get dressed so we can head out. The party has already started."

I beam at her words and walk into my bedroom. Yes, it's mine. It feels so weird to have a safe space of my own and food whenever I want. That one is my favorite, particularly not having to rely on a man to know when I can have my next meal.

After slipping on the dress, I grab a pair of heels —the twin to the pair Milo has at his house—and smirk as I slide them on.

I've managed to save a few thousand dollars and have started paying rent, even though Letti told me everything is already paid for. This place was her auntie's apartment before she moved somewhere else, so it's basically free.

As I step out of my room, Letti claps, then hands me a shot glass and smiles. "Let's have the best night," she says.

I look at the shot glass and grimace before I take it from her hand. The last time I was fucked-up, I told myself I would never do it again. A few drinks here and there is no big deal, but my being on drugs and alcohol led me to make the wrong decisions.

Seeing the look on my face, Letti says, "Lissie, you don't have to drink if you don't like it."

"It's not that." I hand her back the glass. "I've just never felt safe before," I say, shrugging.

Letti's eyes go soft, and she throws her arms around me. "We can always have fun without alcohol."

"No, I want to. I feel safe with you. And you know I have a few drinks now and then... I had some at Milo's. I just never let myself get drunk anymore. Well, blackout drunk," I say, grinning as she releases me.

"You're safe with me, and I will drink less if you

want to drink more. Or we can not drink at all. I'm good either way, as long as we get out there and shake our asses." She shimmies her hips as she says it.

I laugh at her and agree.

Tonight sounds like a great plan.

We drink way more than we probably should, but it's a good night, nonetheless. At first, I held back, unsure and cautious, but Letti has this vibe about her. She makes you feel safe and secure and doesn't put pressure on you to be someone you aren't. And after a few hours, we're both dancing the night away. Though, when she gets drunk, all she wants to talk about is my relationship with Milo. I don't really know what to say because Milo and I aren't a thing. Yes, he is the only man to ever make me second guess everything, and my feelings for him may run deeper than I anticipated, but there is still no 'Milo and me' as such.

"I just want you happy," she slurs as we dance. I nod my head at her because I know that's what she wants for me. And I wish the same for her.

"I am. At least I think I'm getting there." She

pulls me in for a hug, her arms wrapping around me tightly.

"He's good for you, you know. One day, I will have babies, and we will grow old together, and our kids will be best friends like we are." I can only smile at her through the haze of alcohol.

I hope Letti gets everything she wants and more.

"We should call him," she says, pulling back. "Make him confess his love for you."

I chuckle at her and shake my head. My feelings for Milo are... complicated.

"I reckon he could give you some amazing birthday sex." She wiggles her brows and reaches for my phone. I don't stop her. What's the point? She puts it to her ear, and I don't even know if she can hear anything because the music is loud. She giggles and hands me the phone. I grab one of her hands and pull her from the dance floor and towards the door, but she is not leaving.

"Elizabeth."

"Milo Savage," I say his full name back to him. "Why do you never call me by my surname?"

"Because I know a better surname for you, and when I say your full name, it will be the correct one." I scrunch my nose at his words, having no idea what he means. Letti yells something at me and points to the bar.

"Where are you?" I ask him.

"Riding."

"Okay, so how did you answer?" I say, confused. Clearly, I need water.

"You called, I pulled over."

"Oh, that's nice. Are you riding home?"

"No, we are on our way to a job," he says.

"We?"

"Yes, we... the club."

"Oh God, why did you answer?" I say, baffled.

Letti comes back and holds out a drink for me. I'm already drunk, and I know this is going to end badly.

"Because if you call, I will always fucking answer. Even if I am drowning, you get me?" I don't because Cody always ignored my calls, so I am not used to it.

"Let's dance," Letti yells.

"I have to go," I say. "If I call later, feel free not to answer. I'm drunk." I smile into the phone.

"I'll answer," is all I get back before I hang up.

"Where was he?" Letti asks, pulling me back to the dance floor.

"On a ride."

She smiles big. "Those boys don't even answer their wives' calls when they are on a ride." She pulls back and starts to dance as she yells over the music.

"I'm going to have Mason's babies, and you are going to be my bridesmaid, and we are going to have the best life."

I don't argue with her because even though Letti is always a positive person, tonight, she is extra optimistic, and I hope it rubs off on me.

Early the next morning, my phone dings from the bedside table, and Letti kicks a leg over me in her sleep. As I reach for it, I realize somehow we passed out in my bed. When I see *his* name on the screen next to the message, I drop my phone on my face, hitting my lip. I swear and shake my head as I pick it back up.

Milo: When you drink, do you call all the men you've fucked?

I read it two times.

Did I call him?

I go to my call history and note he is the last one called.

Shit.

I must have.

But what did I say?

I don't reply to his text message as Letti stirs next to me.

But then my phone dings again.

Milo: I can see you read my message, Pretty Lady.

I throw my phone across the room, and Letti sits up at the sound of it thudding on the carpet.

"Shit, sorry."

"What's wrong?" She looks around before her hand goes to her head, the aftereffects of last night hitting her full force. "My head hurts." She groans and lies back down. "We drank way too much last night."

My phone dings again from the floor, and I bite my lip.

"Why is your phone dinging?" She covers her head with the pillow.

"Did I call Milo last night?" I ask. Pulling the pillow away from her head, she seems to think about it for a while before she answers, "Yeah, you called, then later on you FaceTimed him," she says, then adds, "He did not look impressed."

"You *let* me call *him*?" I accuse.

"I think you insisted."

Now my phone starts ringing from the floor.

"Can you at least turn it off? It's too loud," Letti grumbles before pulling the pillow back over her head.

I contemplate not answering it, but when Letti groans again, I get out of bed and pick it up.

Turning my phone over, I see his name on the screen. Pressing accept, his face comes into view. *Shit, FaceTime.* I hang up, but he calls again. And again. Stepping out of the bedroom and shutting the bedroom door so as not to wake Letti any more than I already have, I answer it. As I'm pressing my hands to my hair to flatten my curls from last night, I see his face.

"Stop messing with your hair. You look great." I stop fidgeting and focus on him.

"Are you ignoring me?" he asks.

"No."

"Why are you lying?"

I bite my lip and look away.

"You do know I can see you, right?" I bring my eyes back to his and catch him as he licks the scar on his lip, his gaze assessing me. *How can he be so intimidating even through the damn phone?*

"Why are you awake?" I ask.

"Because you are," he says. "You called last night."

"I don't remember," I tell him honestly.

"I do." He grins. "One of us has to remember you confessing your love for me." I gasp, and he just smirks.

"I did not." I sound horrified, my voice trembling slightly as my cheeks flush.

"No, you didn't."

"Why are you calling, Milo?"

"You know why." I sit down on the couch, tucking my legs up under me and pulling a small blanket over them. "I have to tell you something..." His voice drops low, and he looks away for a second.

"Will it make me sad?" I ask. My head hurts, and

I don't want to deal with anything that might make my heart hurt, too. "Will it make me want to hide?" I whisper.

"Yes."

"Okay, then don't tell me yet. It can wait."

"I still have your book."

"I know."

"You should come over."

"I need more sleep," I tell him.

"You can sleep with me," he offers.

I pull the blanket up over me and cling to it as I hold my phone with the other hand. "Milo..."

"Don't you miss it?" he asks, without even knowing what I'm about to say.

"Miss what?"

"Being with me."

God, I do. I miss him so much. But I don't want to go back down a road where I'm not fully in control.

"I should sleep." I try to smile but fail.

"If you say so," he utters. He moves his phone, and now I see he is not wearing a shirt. My gaze slides down to his chest before moving back up to his eyes. "It was fun to break all those rules, wasn't it? You and me." He winks.

"Very much so," I agree.

Someone knocks on his door. He sets his cell down to answer the door, and I can hear him say something. I wait, holding the blanket to me until I hear his footsteps, and he comes back into view.

"Happy birthday. Open your door," Milo says.

I glance to the front door and back to the phone. "Why?"

"Open the fucking door, Elizabeth," he growls.

I smile as I get up and do as he says. On the floor, outside the door, is a large bag. I bring it inside and shut the door behind me. Placing the bag on the kitchen counter, I open it, and the minute I do, my gaze flicks to his on the screen. He's watching me with those dark, dangerous eyes.

"You get that you're supposed to be a big scary man, right?" I watch as his lips fight a smirk.

"I am," he says proudly.

"Okay, so why are you buying me books?" I lift one out and smile as I read the title.

They're all from the same author of the book he stole from me.

"I have ulterior motives," he says.

"You want me to read them to you," I say, knowing where this is going.

"No, *I* want to read them to *you*. While you sit naked and listen to me." My cheeks flush at his words. "Happy birthday. Be ready tonight... I'm cooking you dinner. And bring one of those books with you." Then he hangs up before I can say another word.

I can't help the smile that plays on my lips as I pull each book out of the bag. In total, there are twenty-six books, matching my age. I don't know if he did that on purpose, but I sure as hell love the thought.

Chapter 29

Milo

"I'd buy her the whole fucking library if I could."

She's waiting outside when I arrive, sitting on the curb and playing on her cell. When she hears my bike, she looks up and smiles, standing and brushing her hands over her pants as she does. When I pull up beside her, I hold out the helmet for her.

Lissie takes it and studies it for a moment. "Whose is this?" she asks. "It looks new." She lifts it to her nose and smiles. "Even smells new."

"It's yours. Put it on."

"You bought me a helmet?" she asks, wiggling her brows.

"Yes. Now, get on." Her smile is contagious as she slides the helmet on and puts her cell into her bra before she climbs on, this time without my help. I take her hands and place them around me so she has to hold onto my belt. My cock twitches at her closeness.

Her body leans against mine and doesn't move the whole ride. I never liked having a passenger. I actually refused to have one—until *her*. But I would have this woman on the back of my bike any fucking day.

We ride to my house, and as soon as we're parked out front, she climbs off and pulls the helmet off, her long black hair flowing over her shoulders.

"Can you actually cook?" she asks.

"Of course I can," I tell her, my eyebrows knitting together in offense.

"Okay, just making sure." She shrugs, and I grab her hand to lead her to the house. When we reach the door, I lift her finger and put it to the lock, and the house unlocks.

Lissie looks at me and says, "I may break in to steal my book back since you refuse to give it back."

"You're in luck. The book is here. But you won't get it until after dinner," I tell her as I walk to the kitchen.

She looks around, as she did last time. "I really love this house," she gushes.

"So do I."

Lissie enters the kitchen as I'm pulling out the steaks I have marinating.

"Can I help?"

"No, you sit. I take it you don't want a glass of wine, considering you drank so much last night."

"Oh, gosh, no. I couldn't think of anything worse right now. Do you have soda?"

I reach into the refrigerator, grab a can, and then hand it to her. Then, I turn on the stove and heat up a pan to cook the steaks. I already have the sides prepared. Once I've got the steaks in the pan, I open the fridge and pull out the salad and pasta.

She looks everything over and smiles. "It smells so good."

"What did you do today?" I ask, glancing over my shoulder at her.

She pushes her hair behind her ear and looks down at the food. "Letti and I got manicures and massages. It was the best. I haven't felt that special since I was a kid," she says. "My mother used to take me to the movies and out for ice cream every birthday. After she died, I never really celebrated my birthday much." She shrugs. "Well, Cody never did either, I guess."

"Why did you even marry him?" I've always

wondered what she saw in that piece of shit that made her want to spend her life with him.

"He was what I thought I needed. He was there for me when no one else was."

"What about your sister?"

She raises her eyes to me with a small, sad smile. "She's good now, but back then, not so much."

"That's why Cody borrowed the money and made you pay it back."

Her eyes go wide. "He told you that?"

"No, but I figured it out after six months of you showing up." I take the steaks off and plate them up, offering her one.

"Why did you agree to it?" she asks, not meeting my eyes. "Did you know I wouldn't sleep with you?"

"I didn't agree. I requested you," I tell Lissie truthfully.

She sucks in a breath, like she can't believe the words, and shakes her head. "What do you mean you requested me?"

"He borrowed money from me, and I gave him the same rules as anyone who borrows from me... I get it paid back with interest or I take it from you. With him, though, I added on the condition that you would visit me."

"You didn't even know me," she says, confused.

"But I'd seen you, and that was enough," I reply. And it was. I knew the minute I saw her that I wanted to know more about her. I wanted her around me in any way I could get her. So when that desperate fuck came and begged for more product and then money, I made a plan.

"I don't know how to take that," she says, looking down.

"Just eat your steak. We have to go upstairs soon and read." I smirk at her.

"Milo."

"Hmm?"

"Thank you." She cuts into her steak.

And I sit here like a fucking stalker and watch her eat.

Chapter 30

Lissie

"The way he says that one word."

He has a chair positioned in front of his bed, and on the mattress is my book and a pair of heels. I look back at him to find him smiling at me.

"I take it you want me to put the heels on?"

He walks to the bed, picks up the book, finds the chapter he wants to read, then sits in his chair and nods to the bed.

"I'll read. You get undressed and on that bed in nothing but those heels." He doesn't wait for me to reply before he starts reading.

"His eyes... Somehow, they see straight through me, like he's looking at a piece of me I've never seen before. His body hovers over me, and he brushes a

piece of my hair off my face as he locks his gaze on mine."

When he stops, I turn my head toward him. He's sitting there with his brow raised, waiting for me to follow his instructions.

I grab the hem of my shirt and pull it off over my head, then shimmy my jeans down my legs until I'm in nothing but my panties. His gaze burns as it runs over me.

"I think it's only fair you do the same," I say as I reach for the heels. "If you want me to wear these that is." I smirk as the heels dangle off my fingers in some sort of sexy taunt.

"What do you want?" he asks.

"Take off your shirt." I nod to it. He carefully places the book back on the bed, stands, and removes his leather vest. Draping it over the back of the chair, he then shucks his shirt and tosses it to the floor. He glances at me before he takes the book and sits back down.

This man is dangerous to my body and mind. I have never felt more wanted or comfortable around another human being than I do with him. There is just something about him I can't fully explain.

He opens the book again, his booted foot coming up and resting on his opposite knee as he focuses on reading the words once more. I sit on the bed and put the heels on as I listen to his voice.

"*I want you, and only you.*" He says the words from the book, but I glance up at him to find his eyes on me. He smirks before he looks back down. "*He says that, but my heart flutters, and I wonder how this man can want me. I know he does, for the simple fact I can feel him hard against me, but he actually wants me. Not just what's between my legs.*" I suck in a breath and lie back on the bed.

"Remove the panties," he orders. I do as he says, lifting my ass and sliding them down my legs before dropping them to the floor.

"Now yours," I purr.

"I'm not wearing panties." His glazed eyes are locked on me.

"Jeans. Remove the jeans."

He licks his lips and stands, kicking his boots and socks off before undoing the buttons. He pulls the denim down his legs and steps out of them.

He stands there, completely naked, his cock hard and his body on full display for me. Just like mine is for him. He sits back down, picks up the book, and opens it again without any hesitation.

"You can just come over here." I tap the bed. "You don't need to read to me." His eyes don't blink as he stares at me. He seems to contemplate my words for a moment before he adjusts the book, holding it above his cock, which is standing tall against his stomach.

I breathe deeply as he starts up again, ignoring my invitation.

"*He spreads my legs, pushing them open with his knees as his hand threads through my hair.*" He stops reading and lifts his gaze to me.

"Spread them," he commands, and I do. He looks between my legs and licks his lips before he goes back to the book.

"*The tug of his fingers in my hair makes me spread them a little bit wider, and that's all he needs before his fingers slide down over my hip and slip between us through my folds and straight to my pussy.*" He stops again.

"Do as I say." I nod at his words and slide my fingers between my legs. He stands, then leans over me, the book still in his hand. I hear him take a deep breath, his nose inches from where my hand is, before his tongue flicks against me and makes me jump. It's quick, just a taste, but it's everything. I push my hips up toward him, but he stands and reads again. "*He slides a finger inside.*" His eyes lift from the book and drop to where my hand is.

I do as instructed, slipping a finger inside myself. He nods before he goes back to the book.

"*His finger on my clit, applying pressure that my body needs before he inserts a second finger, working his magic.*" I don't insert a second finger, and when I don't, he leans down and does so with his own finger, staring at my hands as they work my body—one on my breast, the other on my clit as he pushes in and out of me. A noise leaves my mouth, maybe a moan, as he starts reading again.

"*He whispers something in my ear. Maybe he's calling me a good girl—I can't quite hear it. His fingers are captivating me, and his body's weight is perfect as my hands cling to his sides. He keeps up his slow pace for a few moments, then he stops.*" His hand leaves me, and I groan. I go to sit up, but he shakes his head. "Stay."

"That's unfair," I complain. He smiles and turns to face me fully.

"You read. If you stop, I stop."

I'm confused at first, but when I take the book and look down at the passage, I feel him move between my legs, his hot breath on me. "Start," he commands, then his tongue darts out and licks me. He does it again, and I moan. "Start," he growls against me. I nod and manage to open my eyes and look back at the words. I find where he stopped and pick up from there.

"*I look at him, and he smiles a big smile at me. It takes everything in me not to tell this man that I'm falling in love with him.*" I pause, and his tongue moves a little faster as he inserts his finger. I moan and quickly look back at the book. "*He leans down, and before I can confess anything to him, his lips find mine, and his body applies more pressure as my legs open wider. He slides straight into me, and I pause the kiss, my mouth open, but his lips don't stop moving, and somehow I manage to catch up to him and kiss him back.*"

It's hard for me to concentrate on the words when his mouth is working wonders down below, but I somehow manage to read them. And as I turn the page, he inserts another finger and applies pressure to my clit with his tongue. The book is all but forgotten as I drop it next to me, my hands clutching his white bedspread as a soft moan leaves me.

I feel it.

I'm so close.

So fucking close.

He doesn't stop, and I wonder if he's also forgotten about the book.

My heels dig into his back as I wrap my legs

around him. When I come, he takes one last lick, sending my body into a fucking shock of happiness. It literally feels like I'm coming down from the best high I have ever been on.

"You stopped reading," he says as his hands wrap around my hips. Milo pulls me so my ass is on the edge of the bed, and I can feel him there.

I lean up on my elbows and smile. "Best head ever," I say.

"I should fucking hope so," he retorts and looks between us as he notches himself at my entrance. "Now, inch by fucking inch, you will read me the next page." I look at him, confused, and he nods to the book. "Every sentence gets an inch. And, baby, there are more than six inches."

I feel him there, but he doesn't make a move to push inside. I lie back down and grab the book.

"Good girl," he says as I open the book to a random page. I couldn't care less where we were.

"The way he grips my hair like he's done it a thousand times is my all-time favorite thing in this world, apart from the way he stares at me. That is the best." I look away from the book as he pushes his tip in.

"Read," he demands.

"I just want him to fuck me."

"Was that the book or you?" he asks with a smirk.

I sigh and actually go back to the book.

"His hands are always tender but rough at the same time, never hurting me but rough enough that I love it," I read, then look up at him. He slides in a little further. I feel myself pulsing down there—the need, the hum is everywhere.

It's torturous.

"He whispers in my ear before I feel him right where I need him the most. He doesn't care that people are around. Heck, neither do I." I groan as he moves again.

"Fuck me," I moan.

"I'm trying, but you aren't reading fast enough, Pretty Lady," he says, and his face looks as strained as I feel.

I read as fast as I can this time. *"People are walking by everywhere, and it's the middle of the day, but he doesn't seem to care. I mean, I'm straddling his lap in his car."* He slides in farther. *"I take as much of him as I possibly can before he leans forward and bites my shoulder."* Deeper. *"I start to move on him, and the way he breathes my name through those lips I love to touch is like kryptonite."* I throw the book as he pushes in again and lift my hips to him. He slides the rest of the way in, and I groan in pleasure.

"That's my Pretty Lady," he says as I scream.

The buildup and the pressure get to be too much, and his hips start to move, fast and hard, his fingers on my clit, rubbing small circles over the sensitive bud. A part of me wants to push his hand away, while the other is ready for the explosion I know it's about to give.

He pushes in and then stops. I try to move my hips, and he laughs before he moves again. And this time, he fucks me like he can't get enough of me, and I take it because I can't get enough of him.

When he comes, I do as well.

He falls forward, laying his head on my breasts. "Will have to find a new book soon," he mumbles, and when I turn my head, I can see I've torn the pages and ripped some out.

Chapter 31

Milo

"I'm such a fucking sinner, and I love it."

It wasn't long after we had sex in the shower before she passed out, and I followed close behind her. She rolls over in her sleep now, pressing herself against me, and I pull her in close. Her head nestles on my chest as I trace the tattoos on her back.

I'm low-key obsessed with her.

And I can't fucking help it. Every inch of her is perfect.

I haven't yet seen a side of her I don't want to be around.

"Milo," Lissie mumbles my name. "I have to go. I didn't plan to stay." She yawns but doesn't open her eyes or move to get up. "I have to see the lawyer today. Mason set me up with her." I know Mason did because it was my idea, and it is my lawyer. It's why Elizabeth is basically getting the service for free.

"But you don't have to go now," I say and pull her on top of me.

She comes easily, her hands resting on my chest as she looks up at me. "I do, and I'm sore." She winces. I smirk as she blushes. "Can you take me home?" she asks, hopeful.

"Yes, but I'll bring you right back."

"This one-night stand isn't really working out as I thought it would," she says, smiling, and gets up. She finds her clothes and begins getting dressed. We showered last night and then promptly fell asleep together.

Best fucking night ever.

I watch as her jeans slide over her ass, and she glances at me, her cheeks getting even redder as she notices my hard cock.

"I would say it's normal, but we shouldn't lie to each other." I wink.

"Milo..." she starts. I sit up, grab my jeans, and get dressed, throwing her her shirt when I find it mixed in with my clothes. She slides it on. "You know I plan to leave town, right? There is nothing here for me. I need..." she looks around, searching for the word she wants, "... freedom. I've never really had that before."

"Yeah, freedom," I say. "You deserve it." She smiles and comes up to me, gripping my hips. Lifting up on her tiptoes, she tries to kiss me, so I bend down to reach her lips, cupping her chin.

"Thank you for not asking me to stay. I'm afraid I'll say yes."

"I'm afraid I'll ask." I touch my lips to hers before I can say another word.

She deserves everything, and if I'm not a part of that everything, I guess I need to learn to live with it.

No matter how fucking hard it will be, no matter knowing no woman will ever compare to her.

Fuck my morals.

What I have left is just for her.

Chapter 32

Lissie

"I'm rich."

 M ilo takes me home and lingers longer than probably necessary. But Letti was already waiting, as I asked her to come with me to the lawyer's office. It's not my lawyer I'm seeing, though, which has been really confusing. I got a letter in the mail the day before my birthday that was sent to my old address but was redirected to Letti's.

Letti smirks when she sees Milo pulling away as she comes outside and unlocks her car door.

"So... anything you want to talk about?" She wiggles her brows at me.

"No," I say, getting into the car. "But holy hell, who knew sex could be that good."

"Oh, sex is amazing. But when the man knows what he's doing... well, you know."

She starts the car, and I nod. "Though I bet Milo is better than most, he's so..."

I turn to look at her. "He's so what?"

"Scary," she says. "And I've known him most of my life." She pulls out onto the road and drives us to the lawyer's office just outside of town. Letti has somehow become like a guardian angel, one I never saw coming but am so thankful for.

"Should I come in with you?" she asks as I stare at the tall building.

"Would you mind?"

The letter didn't tell me exactly why I needed to be here, only that I had to come to settle some old debts from my mother. At least, that's what I took from the letter.

Getting out of the car, Letti comes over and grips my hand as we head to the building. I give it a squeeze before I let it drop as we walk inside. We take the elevator up to the tenth floor. When the doors open, I approach the receptionist and give her my name, and she guides us to an office. Letti stays by my side as we sit, and the man in front of us offers us a kind smile.

"It's lovely to meet you. I was your mother's

lawyer a long time ago," he mentions. "I guess you're probably wondering why you're here," he says, and I nod. "I've actually been trying to reach you, but your husband said everything can go through him. Of course, I told him that isn't how it works." I glance at Letti as she shakes her head.

He continues, "You turned twenty-six yesterday. Happy belated birthday. I asked to meet you because your mother left instructions for me to pass on a letter to you when you turned twenty-six."

His words hit me.

Hard.

My mother? I don't understand. *She's dead.*

He begins reading...

My little Lissie,

I'm not feeling well, and I'm sorry for that. I have made bad decisions in this life, but there was one that I never did wrong. And that was you. Gosh, how perfect you are. I'm sorry everything had to end like this. I'm sorry for everything. But you see, sometimes when someone is sick, nothing can help them.

I wanted your twenty-sixth birthday to be special because mine was. It was when I found out I was pregnant with you. The day before, your father left me and went back to his wife. He told me he would leave her, but he never did. I was hanging on by a string when I took that test. You saved me, Lissie, but in the end, I was just too broken.

Please take this money; it's all the payments from your father. I kept every cent for you. I love you so much. Please always remember that.

Love,

Mom.

When he's finished, he slides the letter over to me. I take it. I see it's her handwriting, and attached is a photo of her and me when I was one.

I have no photos of her.

How have I not realized that before?

I pick it up and wipe away the tears that have started to fall. I can't stop them.

"Elizabeth." I look up to the lawyer. "Here is the check."

He hands it to me, and I look down at it, wiping my eyes, as Letti breathes out the words, "Holy fucking shit."

I gasp. *No. Fucking. Way.*

"It seems your father was rich and willing to keep you a secret," the lawyer adds.

"Do you know anything about him?" I ask.

He shakes his head. "I'm sorry, no." He pauses.

"But I do know a good private investigator," he says with a smile.

Letti gets all the information as I sign some forms, and soon, I'm walking out holding a check worth a lot of money—seven figures.

I can leave.

I can finally leave.

I went straight to the bank.

No stops.

And now Letti is sitting in front of me, opening a bottle of wine.

"Do you think the investigator will find anything?" I ask, reaching for the glass.

"I hope so. It would be good for you to know who he is, you know?" She shrugs. "But even if he comes up with nothing, you'll still have me." Her smile is so warm and tender that I wish I would have become friends with her sooner. I wish I had people like her around when I needed them, and not Cody.

My phone rings, and we both look at it. The screen shows a private number.

"Answer it," she says.

"It could be Cody," I reply, biting my bottom lip.

"Or, it could be another check." She wiggles her dark brows.

Picking it up, I press accept, and the detective's voice comes through. "Lissie?" I nod, then realize he can't see me. "Yes, here, sorry."

"I found him. He didn't do a good job of hiding, so that task was straightforward." He starts to rattle off information, and I realize he only lives six hours away. I look to Letti, who is grinning.

"Did you talk to him?" I ask.

"Yes," he says. "He would like to meet with you."

"Meet?" I squawk. "Okay…"

The detective tells me my father's information and that he would like to meet in a week if I can. I thank him and hang up the phone.

"So, we need a plan," Letti announces.

"Letti." I sigh. She already has a pen and paper out, ready to start.

"Yeah?"

"I think I'm going to leave," I whisper, not believing the words that leave my mouth.

"Leave? Like a break?"

"No, like I think I want to leave town. Actually, I know I do. Nothing is holding me here anymore. I think I want to just go, and I have the money to do so now. I have never been in a position to do that before.

What money I did have, I either gave to Cody, or he took it," I say in a rush.

"It's not that I don't plan to come back one day. I would still want to see you. I think you are probably the best thing that's happened to me in a long time."

She holds up her hand to stop me from talking. "Don't explain yourself to me, Lissie. I'll be sad to see you go, of course. But I've watched you over the years. You have been a shell of a person, and to get to know the real you... well, it's been amazing. Wherever you end up, I'll be visiting," she says with a smile.

"Thank you."

"Now, who's going to tell Milo?" Just as she says his name, a knock sounds on the door, and Letti walks over to open it.

I see Mason on the other side. He nods to me before he leans down and places a kiss on Letti's lips. I turn away and look back down to my cell as Mason speaks, "Lissie." I turn back to him. "Milo is hunting your husband," he says, and my eyes go wide. "He didn't make payment and skipped town. I was sent here to ask you if you've seen him."

"No, I haven't," I say, shaking my head. "Where is Milo?"

"He'll be back later. He's following a lead."

A lead that might take him straight to my husband, I guess.

"Thanks," I say as he kisses Letti again.

I head to my bedroom and sit on the bed, feeling the weight of the decision ahead. I start searching for plane tickets to my father, unwilling to endure a six-hour drive. After a few minutes of scrolling, I find a one-way flight leaving tomorrow. Booking it feels like the first step in a long journey ahead of me.

The check should clear in a few days, and I do have money saved. Fuck it!

Cody has clearly moved on, and I guess I have as well.

After buying the ticket, I press call, and Milo answers straight away. "Did you find him?" I ask, lying back on my bed.

"No. Any idea where he would be?"

"Maybe his mother's, but I doubt it," I tell him honestly. She always hated me, thinking I was the issue when it was always him.

"Hmm..." is all I get in return.

"Milo." I hear the deep hum he makes at his name. "I'm leaving tomorrow. Thought I would let you know."

He goes quiet for a moment before he says, "I'm out of town. I won't get back until tomorrow."

"I wanted to say goodbye in person, but I guess over the phone is how we will have to do it," I tell him.

He doesn't respond right away, and I think he's hung up. "Goodbye, Elizabeth," he finally says in a whisper.

Then the phone goes dead.

"Move over." My body is gently nudged in the early hours of the morning. I wake slightly to feel Milo climbing in behind me. I know it's him, without a doubt. His arms wrap around me, and he pulls me to him tight. As he grips me for dear life, I feel he has taken his shirt off but still has his jeans on.

"You're here."

"Rode all night," he says into my hair. He brushes it aside, and I feel him kiss my neck. "Sure am going to miss you, Pretty Lady."

I smile sadly. "I found my father," I tell him. "Well, kind of. I'm meeting with him next week, so I just want to go now and find a place to stay and set up a little."

"You don't have to explain yourself to me."

And something in my chest hurts at his words.

"Milo, I'm sorry if I hurt you."

"You didn't," he replies, and I push myself back into him a little more. "Now, go to sleep. I'll take you to the airport tomorrow."

It's not long before his breathing evens out, and I hear him softly snore as he holds me tight.

My decision weighs heavy on me as I drift off to sleep.

Chapter 33

Milo

"Pretty Lady, I'll miss you."

When I wake, she's already up and ready, coming back into the bedroom in jeans and a knitted sweater, her long black hair tied up. She smiles at me when she notices I'm awake.

"I didn't want to wake you, but I do have to go," she says.

I look around the room and notice it's now empty of her things. I'm not even sure she had much to begin with.

"I'm rich. Did I tell you that?" She beams at me, and a part of me is so fucking mad that she's so fucking happy to be leaving. While the other part would never do anything to hold her back.

Pushing the blankets off, I swing my legs to the

side of the bed before I stand. Reaching for my shirt that I threw on the floor last night, I put it on and then face her. "Congrats," is all I can manage to say.

"Did you find him?" she asks in a small voice. "Cody, I mean. Did you find him?"

"No. He's lucky I didn't."

"Don't kill him... if you find him. Please don't, Milo."

"Why do you care if he lives or dies? He was an ass to you," I growl, stepping closer to her because I can't help myself.

"I don't love him, and I don't even like him, but I don't wish for him to die," she says innocently.

I shake my head, not wanting to have this conversation with her. "Let's take you to the airport."

"My bag won't fit on your bike."

"I have a car parked out front."

I grab her suitcase and walk out of the bedroom. Letti is waiting for her, and when she sees me, her eyes widen in surprise. Mason let me in last night and must not have told her.

Lissie follows behind me and goes straight over to Letti, and they fall into a tight hug. I hear a muffled "I'm going to miss you" and "please call" before Lissie pulls back, her eyes glistening with unshed tears. The bond between them is palpable.

Lissie takes a deep breath and steps back. She gives Letti a reassuring smile, though there is sadness lingering in her eyes. "I've never really had a best friend," Lissie says. "And while I have a sister, you feel more like both of those things to me than anyone else." I see her wipe a tear that's fallen from her eye. "Please come visit me," she says to Letti. "I'll pay." She winks. "Since everything you have done for me, it's only fair."

"You paid me back, Lissie," Letti reminds her. "And, of course, I'll come visit. I'll even drag the boys with me." Letti looks past her to me. I just stare at them as I wait at the door, giving them a moment to say their goodbyes before Lissie and I head out to the car. I put her bag in the trunk and then open the passenger door for her. She climbs in, her silence speaking volumes as I start the engine and begin the drive. The quiet between us is heavy, but I can feel her gaze on me. The unspoken tension is hanging in the air between us.

"You've been one of the best surprises. I wanted you to know that," she says sincerely.

I look at her as I pull up at a stop light.

"And you've been amazing in bed." I wink at her. She giggles and shakes her head.

Fuck, I love the sound of that giggle.

"Thank you, though. Will you stay in contact with me?" she asks.

I bite my lip, unable to answer that. But she gets it.

When we pull up to the airport, I get out and grab her bag. Her steps are slow as they bring her to me. "Milo."

"Yes?" I answer her, feeling like this is our final goodbye.

And I fucking hate it.

I hate the way it makes me feel.

The way her leaving affects me more than anything.

"Kiss me?" she asks.

Placing the bag on the ground, I wind my arm around her back and pull her to me.

She comes easily, and our bodies are flush when my lips find hers.

No matter what, and no matter how hard I tried, I don't think I could refuse kissing Elizabeth Petal.

The minute she started reading to me all that time ago, I was hooked.

The minute she stepped into my space, I was a goner.

And all the while, she had that piece of shit who didn't ever see her.

Holding her face with both hands, I deepen the kiss. She kisses me back, her hands fisted in my shirt, clinging on. People honk around us, but I couldn't care less. Smiling against her lips, I pull back but remain close enough to still breathe the same air as her.

"I'm sure going to miss you, Pretty Lady," I tell her truthfully.

"I'm going to miss you, Milo. Thank you." I know I should let her go, but my hands are still attached to her face. "Please visit me. I would love to see you again."

I release her, saying nothing but "Goodbye, Elizabeth." Then, I get into the car before I do something fucking crazy and make her stay.

Chapter 34

Lissie

"Beg me, please."

y sister meets me when I land, her eyes welcoming. She took the week off after I called her the night before to tell her everything. The conversation had been difficult, with long pauses and raw emotion that our mother didn't leave her anything. I offered her some of the money, but she refused. "It's only fair," she said, her voice steady despite the hurt. "I wasn't raised with you, and I didn't share the same struggles. The money is yours."

The whole flight, I thought about Milo. The way he looked at me when I said goodbye, to the kiss that I think will linger for many days to come. I am constantly touching my lips, unable to stop myself.

"Lissie," Savannah squeals, throwing her arms

around me. "I can't believe you actually left. Every time I tried to get you to visit me, you always said no." She laughs and pulls back. "How did it feel, your first flight?" She picks up my bag and heads for the doors.

"Good. When did you arrive?"

"Just an hour ago. Thought I would hang around until you arrived. Ready to check in to the hotel?"

I nod as we walk out and get into a cab.

When we arrive at the hotel, I check in, and then we go up to the room.

"Do you plan to tell me about what happened?" she asks.

I sit on the bed, tucking my feet under me, as I check my cell. I only see messages from Letti telling me how much she misses me already.

"I left him," I tell her.

"Okay, yeah, I get that. But what made you *finally* leave him?"

What was it that finally pushed me over the edge? I think it was a bit of everything. Finally seeing myself, realizing I was more than what he thought I could be, that I deserved to have more in life than just being a wife who barely survived, is the biggest reason.

I smile at Savannah and say, "We didn't love

each other. I think I stayed partially for the fact that he was all I had after our mother died."

She hangs her head and wrings her hands in her lap as she says, "I'm sorry you felt that way. And I'm sorry I was such a shit sister."

"It wasn't on you," I remind her. "And I'm doing good now." I place my hand over hers and give a gentle squeeze.

We order room service and talk most of the night. I told her about Cody, how we stopped kissing and touching each other ages ago, and that it was bound to happen. She confessed that she never liked him but was thankful for his help when she needed it.

I say nothing on *that subject*.

Savannah asks me about my father. I told her that I had hired a private investigator, and when he found him, I searched for him on Facebook. He has two other kids—teenagers, possibly even adults now. I have a brother and sister that I knew nothing about.

That kind of hurts.

The following two days, we explored the city.

And by the weekend, it was finally time to meet my father.

* * *

When I walk into the restaurant, I see a man who looks so familiar to me, even though I've never met him. My sister is waiting at the hotel. I told her I wanted to do this alone, and at first, she was unsure, but I felt it was just something I had to do.

"Elizabeth?" he says, standing as I approach his table. He's dressed in a very elegant suit and is the only man sitting by himself. "You look so much like her," he adds, and my heart hurts a little when he says that. My mother had no family and hardly any friends. Those friends she did have disappeared after I got with Cody, so to hear that I look like her warms something inside of me.

"It's just Lissie. Everyone calls me Lissie," I tell him.

He nods and waves for me to sit.

I pull out a seat and put my bag in my lap nervously. My cell dings and I clutch it in one hand as I grip my bag with the other.

"It's nice to meet you." He sounds a bit nervous, his voice slightly wavering as he fidgets with his hands on the table.

"To be honest, I didn't even know who you were until recently," I tell him. "She never spoke of you." He scratches his cheek, and I notice his short stubble is graying, but he looks good. I would guess he's in his late forties, but I know he's in his fifties.

"I have two other children," he blurts, which I already knew thanks to stalking him on social media due to the PI that found him. "I told them about you, and they would like to meet you if you're up for that." My thumb swipes up and down my bag strap. "My wife is also excited to meet you," he adds.

"Why did you never reach out?" I ask.

He sighs. "I was scared. Your mother was a lot like a roller coaster. And while I was on the ride, I enjoyed it. But when I got off and back to real life… well, that was different." I look at him, confused.

"My wife was angry at me for years, so I stayed away. She knew I sent your mother money but never really said much else, and, to be honest, I was afraid if I brought you up to her again, she would want to leave me, as it would remind her of the mistake I made." I hone in on only one word "mistake," and he notices me bristle. "I don't think of *you* as a mistake, Lissie. My *judgment* was the mistake." I suck in a breath and nod.

"A few years back, I tried to reach out to you, but your husband told me to stay away, that you never wanted to know me, and that if I ever contacted you, he would call the police and put a restraining order on me." He takes a breath. "I didn't want to fuck up your life more than I already did."

What he says about Cody shocks me. *Why did I never know about this?* I would not have turned him away. I needed someone other than Cody.

Though I am partly to blame for that, let's face it, so I can't be angry.

"I'm divorcing him. Our marriage wasn't good. And at the time, he was all I thought I had," I manage to say.

"I'm sorry." Those two little words are filled with regret, and they heal a small part of me.

Like I wasn't the one people ran away from.

That they had to escape.

I *wasn't* the problem.

I hold back the tears at the realization and smile at him. "How old are your kids?"

"Rebecca is eighteen, and Jackson is twenty." His smile is so large when he talks about them, and I can tell he's proud of them. "Rebecca is deciding what she wants to do in this life. And Jackson? Well…" He shrugs. "At first, I thought he wanted to take after me and go into finance, but then he changed and took all his savings and invested in a business. He owns a motorcycle shop. He loves them." Motorcycles will forever remind me of the man with chocolate eyes, whose lips I still feel tingling on mine.

We talk for another few hours before I decide to leave, with a plan to meet the rest of his family—*my* family, I guess you could say. He tells me I don't have to, that it could just be us getting to know each other for now. But I have family now, more than just Savannah. I would love to know them.

On my way to the hotel, I check my cell and find a picture of my books, sent from Milo with the caption, *Read to me...*

I smile the whole way back.

"So, he's nice?" Letti asks a few days later. If I don't reply to her texts within a few hours, she calls.

"Yes, and his family is so lovely. I honestly thought his wife wouldn't like me. But she was so kind," I tell her as I'm lying on the bed. Savannah is getting ready to leave to go home. "Have they found him?" I whisper to Letti.

"No, they haven't, but Milo will. I have no doubt." I chew on the skin of my lip. "I think he misses you," she says cautiously. When I don't reply, she changes the subject.

"Mason asked to move in with me."

"Really? What did you say?"

"That I'll think about it. I don't want to rush anything, you know?"

"I do." It's why I had to walk away from Milo. The old me would have stayed and done whatever he asked; I know that. But now I have changed and won't do what others want me to do just because they can manipulate me.

"Do you plan to stay there?" she questions.

"I'm going to stay for a few weeks at least, then maybe do some traveling. I have this money now, so why not."

"Hell yeah," she agrees.

"Want to come to Thailand with me?" I ask. "My treat."

"Oh my God, are you kidding?" she screams. "When should I pack my bags?"

I laugh. "I have to get a passport first, but I will expedite it."

For the first time in a long time, my life feels like it's *mine*.

Fuck, I love that feeling.

Chapter 35

Milo

"Hunted."

We've been keeping an eye on his house, but he hasn't shown up for a while. His mother, on the other hand, is currently standing in front of me with her arms crossed over her chest, glaring at me.

"*You*," she seethes, looking me up and down. "My son told me about *you*. How you're obsessed with his wife." She makes a weird tsking sound with her tongue. "I told him not to marry her. Look at the trouble you have caused." She shakes her head.

"Where is he?" I ask, trying to keep my cool.

"As if I would tell you that," she scoffs, scrunching her nose up. People are out and staring as I stand toe-to-toe with her, though she's a lot shorter than me. "My son is good, and you are..." She looks me up and down again. "*Not.*"

Morris laughs behind me and shakes his head, and her glare shoots to him, making him laugh even louder.

"I don't know what you're laughing at. You've made this town cheap with your biker ways. It's so much less because you are in it."

"Mrs. Petal," I begin, then lean in so only she can hear. "Your precious son is a drug dealing, whore pimping fucker who owes me a *lot of money*." I pull back. "Be sure to tell him that I want my money back."

Her eyes go large, and she gasps as her hand covers her mouth. "H-he works in construction. He said you had troubles," she stutters.

"Yeah, constructing fucking drugs," Morris mutters.

She turns her shocked expression on him. "He said his wife will have the money," Mrs. Petal says.

Does Cody know about Elizabeth's money?

Fuck, I hope not.

"Make that girl pay it."

"I think she has paid enough of his debts, wouldn't you say, Mrs. Petal? And if he doesn't pay, I will be visiting *you*." I wink at her and slide my sunglasses on before I stalk off. She says something else, but I don't listen.

I pull my cell out and send Lissie a picture of the inside of the book that I will not be returning, and when she replies, something inside of me eases, knowing that her *fuck of a husband* hasn't found her.

I miss you too, is the message she sends back.

"I take it that's Lissie," Morris says. I sit on my bike and slide my cell back into my pocket. "I like her, man, but Cody would already be dead if it weren't for her."

He's right.

I know he is.

So now it's time to stop playing with emotions and get my fucking work done.

"You know, it leads to others thinking they can have the same treatment," Morris adds.

"I know," is all I say.

And I do.

Chapter 36

Lissie

Six months later...

I haven't been back to my hometown.

And I don't intend to go back anytime soon.

Letti is due to arrive any minute, and Mason and Milo will be with her. I have a small apartment with two bedrooms, though I haven't fully furnished the spare room yet. So I went out and bought a bed for it, now that I have friends coming. That feels weird to say in my head. I'm not used to having close friends, but Letti is exactly that—my closest friend—and I hope she'll meet my sister and brother, who I have hung out with regularly. My father, who I am not comfortable calling "Dad" just yet, has been trying, and his wife is actually the sweetest lady ever. Her kids are proof of what a great human she is by how kind they are. Rebecca looks a little like me, whereas Jackson looks exactly like their mother. It's been nice getting to know them. I didn't realize I missed having a family until I finally had one.

There's a knock on the door, and I startle. I take a moment to calm myself down and then go answer it. I'm tired. I've been working at a local bar for the last few months. I fix a smile on my face, take a deep breath, and grip the doorknob. When I pull the door open, arms surround me, and Letti tackles me in a hug before I can even say a word.

"Oh my gosh, I almost died," she says dramatically.

"You did not," Mason says, stepping past us. "Hey, Lissie." He nods, holding her bag.

"What happened?" I ask.

"Turbulence," mutters Milo, standing back, hesitating.

"The worst," Letti adds.

"Yeah, so bad that she dumped her steaming hot coffee over us," adds Mason from behind me as he places the bags down.

"Is anyone hurt?" I ask, hugging her tighter.

Letti pulls back and huffs. "Who cares about

them, it's me who's hurt. Milo had the window seat and would joke about a bird flying into the thingy that flies the plane on the side." She waves her hand around, then steps out of my view so I'm now facing Milo.

"You can come in," I say, opening the door wider in invitation.

He looks me up and down. It's then I realize I forgot to change out of my work clothes. I'm dressed in a pencil skirt, with stockings that have a pinstripe at the back, and a black blouse that is partly unbuttoned. My hair is tied up in a tight bun on the top of my head. The bar where I work is high class, and we are required to dress in the proper attire. His gaze falls to my heels, and the corner of his lips lifts in a smirk.

"Nice heels."

I lift one slightly toward him.

"Told you I had a pair." I grin at him. We've kept in contact in the months I've been gone, but it got less and less as we got busier and busier. But I still see him every night when I close my eyes.

"I see that." He finally steps inside, and I shut the door behind him.

"You two can have the spare room. Sorry, it's small." I open the wooden door to the second bedroom. "New sheets and mattress. Hopefully, it's comfortable," I say as Letti and Mason walk in.

"This is really cute, Lissie. You decorated it all yourself?" she asks, looking around.

"I did," I say, pride lacing my words.

I leave them to it and find Milo wandering around. He stops at some photos on the wall. One is of me and Letti from our trip to Thailand. All the rest are photos I took when I traveled to other places like Japan and Indonesia.

"I have two options for you," I tell him, and he turns to me.

He's dressed in black jeans and a dark gray shirt that showcases his beautiful muscles, and it's weird not to see him in his leathers, but it's refreshing all the same.

"Options?" He raises a brow, and his lips lift, his scar moving with it. "Interesting," he mutters.

"I have this couch, though I can say from experience it's not all that comfortable." He glances at it, then back to me.

"I've slept on worse." He shrugs.

I bite my lip and shift my gaze away from him. "Or my bed," I manage to say. It feels like a pin could drop, and everyone would hear it. I wasn't sure if I was going to offer him that, but after seeing him, I knew I would. He steps closer—one step is all he takes—and he invades my space.

"Which do you prefer?" he asks, the timbre of his voice low and sexy, and I shiver.

"My room."

He sweeps a hand in that direction and says, "Lead the way." I can feel him behind me as I open the door and step inside. He follows me in and places his bag on the floor in front of the bed.

"Lissie," Letti calls, and I poke my head out of the bedroom door to see her opening the fridge. "I'm starving. I haven't eaten because I was too nervous. Can we eat?"

"Yep, let me get changed. There's a cute Mexican restaurant down the road within walking distance that serves the best tacos." I smile, and she claps her hands and runs to her room. She is so happy that it makes me warm inside.

I go back into my room and shut the door behind me, and I see Milo sitting on the edge of the bed. As I walk to my closet, I feel the heat of his stare all over me. It's like fire licking my skin but it's too dangerous to touch. I unbutton my top and discard it in my laundry basket, then I do the same with my skirt, shimming it down my legs, before removing my stockings. Now, all I have left on is a matching pink

G-string and bra. I don't dare turn around as I reach for a clean shirt. Slipping it on, I turn for my drawers and pull out a pair of jeans, and it's then I see his dark, hooded eyes locked on me.

"Dangerous game, Pretty Lady," he growls, standing, his hands at his sides and his tongue sliding over his teeth.

"I remember how you like to play games." I wink at him before I pull on my jeans.

"Only with you." He lifts a hand to touch me, but he stops with it in mid-air before he lets it drop. *I hoped he would touch me.* He glances at the closed door. "We should go. Your friend is hungry and can be very annoying when she wants something." He saunters to the door and holds it open, those ravenous eyes assessing me, eating me up.

"Are you hungry?" I ask him, and his hand tightens on the handle as he looks me dead in the eye.

"That's a loaded question," he answers as Letti appears.

"You two ready? I'm starving." I give a quick "yep" and grab my jacket as Milo waits for me. Walking past him, I catch his sandalwood scent—it floats everywhere around him.

Leading us out, I shut and lock the door, and

then we make our way down the street to the restaurant. Letti places an order without even looking at the menu, including drinks, as soon as we're seated.

"Everything going good with you two?" I ask Mason and Letti.

Mason pulls her into a one-armed hug and kisses the top of her head. "Yep. Though I know to never fly with her again. She's a freak," he says, making her face go red.

"I'm not *that* bad." She looks to Milo for help, and he holds up his hand and turns it over, revealing claw marks. Letti's eyes go wide, and she covers her mouth. "Okay, well, maybe the next time, it won't be as bad."

"I don't think it works like that." Mason chuckles. "I thought Lissie was exaggerating when she said you were a bad flier, but I stand corrected."

I disguise my smile by covering my mouth, knowing she was terrible to fly with.

Our food and drinks arrive shortly after. Mason and Lissie are across from Milo and me. I notice Milo's hands on the table, both of them closed in fists as Mason speaks, and not once does he look my way.

"So, tell us. Letti mentioned some of the things you've been up to, but not everything." Mason smiles as Letti puts a taco to her mouth and bites into it.

"Family, work."

I feel Milo's eyes on me.

"How's the club? I haven't asked because, to be honest, I didn't want to. But have you found Cody?" My question is directed at both Milo and Mason.

Neither answers me.

Milo picks up his cell and starts sending messages. I say nothing more on the subject as we continue to eat our food and make small talk.

Milo doesn't ask me anything at all.

And to say I'm getting a little annoyed with him would be an understatement.

His cell dings a few times throughout dinner, and he doesn't excuse himself once or ignore it; he just continues to pick it up and type. I don't bother asking him who he's speaking to. I just sit there, getting angrier and angrier. At one point, Letti tries to bring him into the conversation. He nods, and that's as good as it gets. I know Mason won't say anything because, technically, Milo is his boss, though I'm not really sure how all that works. I just know that despite him being the big, scary man that everyone thinks he is, to me, he never has been.

"I'm tired." Milo finally speaks.

We've all finished our meals, and I'm on my second margarita.

"I could use a good sleep," Letti agrees, leaning her head on Mason's shoulder.

Milo pays the bill without even asking, and we all get up to leave. On the walk back, he stays next to me but says nothing, and Mason and Letti are behind us, hand in hand.

When we arrive at the apartment, Letti kisses me goodnight before she heads to the guest room with Mason. I walk to my room, and Milo follows. He kicks off his shoes next to the bed as I grab my pajamas and head for the shower. I let him be the whole time, wondering why he hasn't touched me or spoken more than a few words to me.

Does he not *want to be here?*

Is he with someone else?

Maybe I should have asked that question before inviting him into my bedroom.

All these thoughts run rampant through my head.

As soon as I'm clean, I wrap a towel around myself and pull open the door to find him climbing into my bed, wearing only a pair of boxers. His eyes find mine, and he pauses.

"Are you with someone?" I blurt out. One brow raises, and he looks at me as if I've gone mad. *Maybe I have.* "You aren't, right? I mean, I doubt you'd be sleeping in my bed if you were." He shakes his head, and I take that as his answer before I shut the bathroom door, finish getting dressed, and comb my hair. Turning the light off, I step out and climb into bed. I listen as I lie down and hear a soft snore.

He fell asleep.

Without saying one word.

Chapter 37

Lissie

"Can I smother him in his sleep?"

Tossing and turning, I lie there for what feels like hours. I'm mad at him. How could he come out here to see me and not want to talk to me? Did I do something that I'm unaware of? I mean, I don't think I did, but who knows?

I feel the heat from his body as he lies dead-still on his back next to me. My hands are itching to reach out and touch him, but I'm not sure I want to touch someone who clearly doesn't want to be around me.

So why did he agree to share a bed with me?

He could have gone to the couch.

Maybe I should have only given him the option of the couch.

It would have been easier than dealing with the torture of him lying next to me.

"Your thoughts are so damn loud," he grumbles.

"Yeah, well, you're annoying," I snap before I turn over to my side and give him my back.

"Pretty Lady." I ignore him. "We can't do anything until we talk. I have something to tell you. But I don't want to tell you yet because it will ruin this vacation. For everyone."

I huff. "So you decided it was smart that we share a bed?"

"As I recall, that was *your* idea. And, of course, I'm going to pick sleeping next to you rather than on a couch."

So he's here to visit me to tell me something, but he refuses to do so until the end because he doesn't want to ruin our weekend? That seems a bit selfish. I'm not going to lie and say I didn't think that we would sleep together in more ways than one.

I have missed his touch.

I have dreamed of it.

And I was greatly looking forward to having it again.

I hate that he's ruined me for all other men without even knowing he did so.

When I agreed to go back to his house that first

night, I didn't think this would be the outcome—that a few nights with him would have me hooked. I wasn't aware that you could crave a single touch as much as I crave his.

It should be illegal.

Tossing and turning, I'm only getting madder with each passing second. I hear him breathing next to me, and before I explode, I turn to face him. He turns his head to the side and looks me dead in the eye. "You are the most beautiful thing I have ever seen. I've known that since the moment I first saw you," he finally says.

And that's all it takes.

Before I can stop myself, my hand is on his face, feeling the slight stubble before my lips move forward and come crashing down on his. He doesn't pull away, and he doesn't waste any time kissing me back. Our lips move hungrily. He's holding back, but when I want something, I'll take it.

Still cupping his cheek, I crawl on top of him until both my hands are on his face and I'm straddling him. I settle myself over him and feel all of him beneath me. It's evident he wants me as much as I want him.

Fuck what he has to say to me—I couldn't care less right now.

Our bodies want exactly the same thing. At least one of us has to admit it.

His hands grip my hips, and I feel his fingertips digging in as if he's trying to restrain himself, but that's the last thing I want him to do, so I start grinding. I never said I was a good girl. I want him to do bad, bad things to me, and I'm desperate for him to do them right now.

I haven't been with anyone since him.

I love that I can kiss him as easily as it is to breathe air. Our lips haven't broken apart, my hips are moving with more urgency than ever before, and I'm sure his fingers are about to leave marks on my skin.

I move my hands from his face, moving them down until I hit his chest, and then I drag my nails down until they reach the waistband of his boxers. He tries to break the kiss. I guess I can tell he wants to say something, but as he moves his lips, I just follow them with my own. He huffs and grabs my face, kissing me with so much fucking hunger that I'm sure my lips are going to be bruised after this.

His tongue slides into my mouth, and it dances with mine. With the distraction of the kiss, I manage to pull down the waistband of his boxers. All I have on is a nightgown and a thin pair of cotton panties.

As soon as I free him, I wrap one hand around his shaft and start stroking. He swears against my mouth and breaks the kiss. When he pulls back, those dark eyes lock on mine, and I see the heat, the danger that lurks behind them. But it does nothing to stop me. I'd gladly dance with any of his devils, and when I'm done, I'll sit on their faces so they can tell me what a good girl I am.

"You don't know what you're doing." He groans. But as he says it, his lips touch mine again. "I tried to be good, to do the right thing—"

"Fuck the right thing. Fuck me already, Milo." I see a spark in his eyes as my words register, and he tries to shake his head again, but I just tighten my hand around his cock, which makes him hiss. Before I know it, he has the blankets off both of us, and then, in one swift movement, his arm wraps around my lower back, and he flips me so I'm under him with my legs wrapped around his waist. I giggle at the action, and a sinful, sexy smirk appears on his lips at the sound.

He reaches for my nightgown and slides it all the way up my body, ever so slowly, taking his time, eyeing each and every piece of me until my tits are exposed. He leans down and places gentle kisses on them before I pull the nightgown off over my head. I try to move my hips upward to reach him, but he merely holds me down with one hand on my lower abdomen and tsks at me.

"Are you sure?" he asks, just before he leans down and sucks my nipple into his mouth. I nod like a madwoman in answer. "I don't have a condom, but I'm clean," he says. "Last time I was with someone…" When he pauses, I stiffen, waiting for him to finish. "It was you." I relax and beam at him.

"I'm on the pill." He nods, licking his lips before his gaze tracks down to where his hand is on my stomach, just above my panties.

"Well, these will have to go." He pulls the waistband over my hip and releases it, letting it snap back against my skin. "I think I'll keep them, though. You soaked them." His eyes find mind as he drops his head to my panties and bites the side with his teeth. He crawls down my body, taking my trapped panties as he goes.

I lift my leg and let him slip them off, and then he stands and removes his boxers.

And he's naked in front of me.

In all his beautiful fucking glory.

"Are you sure?" he asks again.

"Yes."

"Good." He steps back and takes a seat on my

pink sofa in the corner of the room. I'm sure my expression shows my confusion.

As he sits there, staring at me, he fists his cock and starts stroking it up and down. He licks his lips before he says, "Stand up." I do as he says, then take a step toward him, but he holds up a hand and says, "I didn't say you could move. I said stand up." I halt my movements and wait to see what comes next. "Hands and knees, now." I follow his order. When I'm in position, I see him grip his cock a little tighter, and then he throws my panties at me. They drop in front of me, and he nods to them. "Now pick them up with your teeth and bring them to me."

I would like to say this is the part where I'd get grossed out and tell him to fuck off.

And normal me would.

But horny me? She is a whole different person, and she wants to play whatever game this man wants.

I grab the panties in my hand, and he tsks again.

"Drop them."

"I was going to put them in my mouth," I argue.

"Pick them up with your teeth." I huff and snatch them up between my teeth. When I lift my head, I note he's smiling. "Now, crawl." The hand on his cock pauses its stroking, and he licks his lips.

I take my time as I crawl to him. I feel myself getting wetter at his request. The need to have him is almost overwhelming, and the sight before me as he touches himself is almost too much.

Almost.

When I reach him, he removes his hand from his cock and taps his leg. I sit up on my knees, and he leans forward and takes my panties with his mouth, right in the crotch area. I see his devilish smirk peeking out from behind the material.

"What do you want?" he asks, holding my panties in his hand. "Use words." He drums his fingers on his leg.

"You," I say, but my gaze falls to his cock.

"No, you don't. What do you really want?" he asks again, more insistent this time.

"I want to sit down on that and move," I manage to get out.

"And what is *that*?" He reaches forward and puts a finger under my chin, lifting it so we are eye-to-eye. "Tell me what you want, and it's yours."

"Your cock," I whisper. "Buried so fucking deep inside me that I forget my own name."

His hand drops from my face, and he sits back, his arms stretching out along the back of the couch.

He nods to his cock and offers, "Take what you want."

At first, I'm not sure if it's a trick, and I hesitate for a moment until I see the seriousness in his eyes. I stand up, then straddle him, holding myself above him. I look down between us and slowly drop my hips until I can feel him at my entrance. I release a shaky breath as the tip enters me, and I can't even look at him right now. I'm too busy concentrating on fulfilling my every need with him. I push down a little farther, and my head drops back, my hair falling over my bare back. My chest pushes forward, and I reach for the back of the couch to brace myself, but instead, I grip his wrists.

"Fucking hell," he mutters, and my head shoots up, and I see his eyes focused solely on my pussy as I drop lower and lower until I take as much of him as possible.

"I—" Words fail me.

"Sit," he growls.

"I—"

"*Sit*," he commands.

I do as he says, taking him all in. I have to adjust to the size of him before I can even think about moving. He leans forward, my hands still clamping on his wrists, and takes my bottom lip into his mouth and bites it gently.

I'm not really sure what it is about Milo, but he consumes me.

He isn't even touching me right now, except for his teeth on my lips, but I can feel him everywhere. I grab his hands and place them on my breasts. Instantly, he cups them, and when my eyes meet his, our noses are almost touching. His eyes trace my face, landing on my lips before they move up and lock with mine again. I wonder what he sees when he looks into my eyes because when I look into his, I see so many possibilities and so much danger, but none of that will keep me away right now.

"Move," he says.

Instead of lifting up and down, I push him back farther into the couch and start to rock my hips. He hisses at the movement but doesn't stop me. His hands play with my breasts before he dips low and takes a nipple into his mouth.

My hands land behind me, on his knees, and my back arches as I rock. He thrusts up, meeting my every move so he can be as deep as possible, but each movement I make hits all the perfect spots. My clit rubs against him with each motion, his cock hitting my G-spot deep inside of me and his hands and mouth working my breasts.

"Quiet, your friend is sleeping," he mumbles around my breast.

Before I can respond, I feel the buildup about to take me, and a small scream starts to let loose. But he's quick. He lifts a hand and covers my mouth with it, muffling the scream, but it still escapes anyway. When I slow my rocking, he puts his other hand on my hip and takes over. And I feel another orgasm rising. That can't be possible, though. How am I just coming down from one to be going back up again?

He doesn't remove his hand from my mouth as he continues. In fact, he rocks me until I'm screaming into his hand yet again. But this time, when I come, it is more intense than the last time. He leans forward and bites my nipple, making me grab his head and hold him to me. His hand falls from my mouth, and he now has hold of both my hips.

"Your pussy craves me." He leans in to whisper, "Can you feel it?"

And I do.

I feel all of it.

I know when he comes because his mouth finds mine, and he kisses me hard. And he doesn't stop until both of us are spent and done.

"Milo."

"Hmm?" he hums against my lips.

"Don't *not* touch me again," I tell him, and he pulls back and looks at me. He pushes a strand of hair from my face and locks eyes with me.

"It was just as hard for me as it was for you," he admits.

And, somehow, I believe his words.

Chapter 38

Milo

"Sometimes love comes without warning."

It's unfair, really, to fall in love with someone without warning.

Because that's exactly how it feels with her.

Even the distance couldn't stop us.

I love her. *Fuck me.*

Lissie groans in her sleep, and I run my hands through my hair before I manage to get up without waking her and step out of her room. As I'm closing the door, I see her curl herself into a ball.

"Didn't think you would come out at all." I spin to find Mason opening Lissie's fridge and holding a jar full of Nutella. He dips the spoon in and puts it in his mouth. "Did you tell her yet?" Mason asks with a raised brow.

"No." And I don't intend to, but I will before we leave.

"Okay, let me know if you need me to do anything." I nod, opening the fridge and reaching in for a bottle of water. "Letti knows, just so you're aware, and having her not say anything to Lissie has been a struggle," he adds when I pass by him.

"How does she know?" I ask.

He holds up his hands, which are holding the spoon and Nutella. "Not from me. She figured it out."

"So she's guessing?"

"I confirmed it." His eyes drop, and he knows he fucked up.

I go back to the bedroom to find her in the exact same position she was in when I left. Walking over to her bedside table, I set the water down and slide my pants off before getting back into bed. Reaching for her, I pull her into my side, and she comes without waking, curling herself around me.

Is this what a relationship is like?

Falling asleep and waking up with someone?

Because if it is, how the fuck did that fucker ever turn this woman away?

Chapter 39

Lissie

"Can a girl enjoy being smothered?"

I wake, absolutely smothered by Milo.

Somehow, one of his legs is tangled through mine, half his body is lying on top of me, and his head is in the crook of my neck.

And none of this bothers me at all.

I've been lying here like this for ages, listening to him breathe. I passed out not long after I got out of the shower the second time. As soon as I stepped out, he wrapped me in a towel, picked me up, and placed me in my bed, but not before he removed said towel, putting it on the side of the bed before he climbed in next to me. And this is the position I've woken up in. And I'm not mad—at all.

I'm afraid what they all say about me is true and

that, somehow, I'm going to fall for this man. And fall *super hard.*

If I haven't started to already, that is.

I get rid of those thoughts. *Milo is a good time. And that's it, right?*

So why have neither of you said you want to be with each other? I scramble that thought from my head as quickly as it appears.

"There you go again, thinking so loud."

"I can't help it."

He lifts his head, and his hand goes straight between my legs. "I can help with that."

I smirk at him. "I bet you can."

"Lissie, so help me God, if I have to listen to you have sex again, I will find a hotel." A bang comes on the door, and Milo slips in a finger, not even caring as his thumb finds my clit.

"We'll be out soon," Milo yells, not taking his eyes off me. "*You* will be quiet," he whispers. I go to open my mouth, but he shakes his head. "Quiet," he urges, applying pressure. I squirm at his touch and bite my bottom lip to stop myself from making noises, but it's hard, really hard, when I can feel his body heat all over me, and he is doing dirty, sexy things with his fingers.

"Lissie, come on. I want to go out." Letti bangs on the door again.

"Hurry up and come on my fingers, Pretty Lady. You're running out of time," he whispers. Milo applies more pressure, then his mouth latches on to my nipple, and he sucks.

That's all it takes. And I'm gone.

Has this man got the fingers of a God?

"See? Good girl." He removes his fingers from my body, then climbs off the bed, but

I see him put those two fingers into his mouth and suck.

And all I can think is how hot that is.

* * *

The day goes by quickly. I show them around the city. Milo keeps his distance and makes no move to touch me.

And it pisses me off.

But I don't touch him either.

I take them to the zoo. We have lunch, do some shopping, then we have dinner before we arrive back at my apartment.

Both men got stares all day. Even without wearing their leather, they're both very intimidating, especially Milo. If I didn't know him, I'm not sure I would even talk to him. Actually, I would probably cross the road so I don't run into him.

Most of the day, he kept his hands in his pockets. It irritated me, but at the same time, I shouldn't expect him to touch me in public. It's a battle of wills, and I think I might be losing.

"We should go out for drinks," Milo says, looking me dead in the eyes. "We need to talk. *Alone.*"

"Okay, well, that's our cue. Goodnight, and thank you so much for a great day. I loved it." Letti kisses my cheek before she and Mason walk into the guest room.

I turn to look at Milo. "Should I change?"

"You could go out in a brown bag, and I would still tell you you're the prettiest woman in any room." I blush and step closer to him. Cody never once spoke to me like that.

"So why did you keep your hands to yourself all day?" I ask, confused by his earlier actions.

"Let's go get that drink," he says, avoiding the question.

I head out the door, and as soon as we're in the hallway, he grabs my hand and slides his fingers between mine. I look down at our joined hands, then smile up at him.

"You don't like to do it in front of your club members?"

"I couldn't care less about that."

"Okay, so... Letti, then?" He raises a brow. "Then why?"

"I don't do this shit. It's you who wants it," he replies. "And, clearly, you want this." His grip on my hand tightens as we walk.

"You don't enjoy holding my hand?"

We reach the closest bar, and he pulls open the door for me to enter. His gaze tracks my every move, and as I step past him, he leans down and whispers, "I enjoy touching any piece of you, especially inside your pussy as you come."

I know my face flushes, but I keep my grip on his hand and move forward. We find a place at the bar with no one next to us. The bartender comes over, and Milo orders me a wine and a scotch for himself.

"What did you want to talk about?" I ask.

"Not quite yet. Let's have a drink before you hate me."

"Hate you?" I raise a brow. "Did you fuck Letti?" I question, half joking but terrified about his answer at the same time.

His brows pull together, and he stares at me. "Why on earth would I fuck your friend?"

I shake my head, relieved.

"How do you want this to go, Pretty Lady?"

I brush a strand of hair behind my ear. "What do you mean?"

"Us," he says, turning his body to me and placing his hand on my thigh. "I want to know, even though I already know my answer."

"You're making no sense," I say, my brow furrowing. "As for us, I like what we are now. How we are." I smile. "It's... good."

"So every six months, I fly out for the weekend and fuck you?" he asks, just as the bartender sets our drinks down. I offer him a smile, hoping he didn't hear what Milo just said but knowing he more than likely did.

"Savage." I turn to see three men striding our way. They eye Milo before one of them—the one who spoke, I assume—gives me a slow once-over and smirks. "It's you in our neck of the woods, isn't it?" His hand comes down on Milo's shoulder.

"Remove it," Milo orders without hesitation.

The man does, pulling his hand away and then lifting both in surrender.

"Are you here for business?" another asks. Turning to me, he stares at my legs and tits. "Or pleasure?" He winks, finally meeting my eyes.

"Keep your fucking eyes to yourself before I cut them out." I turn from the fool who was staring at me and look at Milo. The Milo sitting before me right now is tense, and I can tell he doesn't want these people's company.

"Hey, hey, brother, we're all friends here," the first guy says. "And you seem to be forgetting where you are," he reminds Milo. I never really understood club business.

Milo slides his tongue over his teeth and sucks in air as a devilish smile touches his lips. "And you seem to be forgetting who the fuck I am. Shall I remind you?" Milo taunts.

The man looks at me before moving his attention back to Milo. "We just wanted to say hello. No harm done." He holds up his hands. "We'll just leave. Have a good night." He nods to Milo and smirks at me before they saunter away.

Milo is quiet as they leave, not turning back to face me until they're gone.

"Who are they?" I ask.

"Assholes" is all he replies. I don't bother arguing, knowing club stuff is his stuff. *I know it's bad, but is all of it? How can he be so bad when, to me, he is anything but?* "Drink. We'll leave after."

I notice the change in his posture, so I lean in and put my head on his shoulder.

"How about I show you how much my tongue has missed you on my knees in my room after this?" I offer.

Those heated eyes find mine, and now they aren't tinged with anger. It's lust. He lifts a hand, and his thumb strokes my brow before he leans in and kisses the edge of my jaw with feather-light kisses.

"Anything with you," he says, and we forget about everything. He makes me forget about everything but him.

His touch.

The way his kisses linger all over my skin, marking it for him.

And the way no other man can compete with this man.

He holds the power, and I'm letting it slip by giving it to him.

"Okay, let's go." I pull away and stand.

Throwing some cash on the counter for the drinks, he grips my hand, and we waste no time leaving. As soon as we step outside, we head in the direction of my apartment. It's not far, and I want to spend every minute with him in my bed before he leaves tomorrow.

Just as we turn the corner, something in the air shifts—it hits differently. I'm not sure how to describe it exactly. But everything changes. A loud *thunk* is all I hear before his hand leaves mine. I turn toward him, confused, to see him doubling over in pain before I notice the three men who just stepped out of the alley behind us.

"Wonder what makes you so special to have the Savage Villains' Prez with you. Killing you will make us kings. No one will fuck with us," one says.

Milo isn't down. He's just bent over. So I move toward him, but before I can reach him, one of the men pulls me to the side.

It all happens so fast—it's almost a blur in front of my eyes. I try to push away from the man, but he simply laughs. He wraps his arm around my waist, pulling my back to his front. I feel his hardness and excitement for me at the struggle, and it disgusts me.

"Let me go." It's almost a scream, but before I can say or do anything else, Milo is standing straight again. He punches the guy to the right of him straight in the gut, making him buckle over. Milo then grips the guy's head and slams it into his knee. You can hear the crunch, sounding a lot like bones shattering.

The second guy is holding a knife, and Milo

takes it from him easily, and in one quick move, he's behind the guy, holding the knife to his neck. It's then he finds me gripped in the arms of the third man.

"Before I slice your throat, I'd suggest you tell your man to remove his hands from the lady." The man with the knife at his throat goes to laugh, but Milo applies pressure, and blood starts to leak around the knife's blade. "Do you know me to be a joking man, Constable?" he asks.

"Let her go," the man with the knife at his neck says. At that moment, I turn around and kick the guy who was holding me straight in his junk.

"Asshole," I grumble and wipe my hands down my jeans while I lock my focus on Milo.

"Now, you know I can't let you go without a warning." Milo pauses. "It would be wrong of me, after all." All three faces go white, but one looks at me as if he's ready to grab me again. "Tsk, tsk. I wouldn't do that if I were you." I step out of reach. And in what feels like three breaths, Milo drops the knife. And before I can see what he's doing, the man is screaming. Milo steps back, and the man turns, revealing the knife now protruding from his ass cheek.

Ouch.

Milo walks over to the other man and uppercuts him straight into his jaw, knocking him backward to the ground.

"Next time, I won't be so polite," Milo tells the men.

He rushes toward me, and when he reaches me, his hand slides into mine. We hear sirens and start moving. Fast. We hurry past my apartment, and I don't even ask why. I know why because they can still see us. We do a slow lap around the block, and when we come back around, the men are gone. Stepping inside, I shut the door and lock it after him. When I turn around to face Milo,

I see blood dripping on the floor.

And that's when I scream, "Mason!"

Chapter 40

Milo

"Forever ruined by her touch, even if I am dying."

The worry etched on her face hurts me more than the knife wound in my stomach.

She rips at my shirt, lifting it up, trying to undress me to see where the blood is coming from.

"I could get used to this." I grin down at her.

Lissie looks up at me with those stunning eyes and narrows them. "This is not something to joke about. You're bleeding."

"I've been stabbed before. Fuck, I've even been shot, Pretty Lady. Yet, here I am, still standing," I say as she points to the couch. "I'll ruin your couch," I tell her. She shakes her head, and I move to her kitchen instead and sit on one of the stools.

I watch as she and Letti try to find the first aid kit.

That's when there's a knock on her door. We all freeze, and Mason walks out of the bathroom with a wet cloth and glances at the door. I pull my shirt down as Mason walks over and pulls it open. Before Elizabeth has a chance to go see who it is, I grab her wrist and pull her back. She looks at me with shocked eyes but nods her head as if she gets my meaning. She will *not* get hurt. Even though I'm certain they didn't follow us, there is no fucking way she will get hurt while I'm alive.

"Umm, who are you?" a man asks.

At the sound of his voice, Elizabeth pulls her hand free, goes straight to the door, and pushes it open farther, revealing two people on the side.

I stand and move so I'm directly behind her.

Two sets of eyes find mine, both the same color as hers.

The guy, dressed in jeans and a white shirt, raises a brow.

"Is this your boyfriend?" the girl asks, pointing at me with a smile.

"No, this is Milo. He's a friend from my hometown—"

"Yes, I'm her boyfriend," I state, interrupting her

as I stare down the guy. I feel her eyes on me. So I turn and see her gaze narrowed at me and her lips pressed in a thin line, clearly in a shitty mood.

"Milo, this is my sister and brother." *Oh.*

"Rebecca and Jackson." She points to each of them. "This is Milo Savage," Elizabeth says to them. "And our friends who answered the door are Letti and Mason."

"Like *the* Milo Savage?" Jackson says, taking me in with a new gleam in his eyes.

He's young, but I see the brand on his shirt, which clearly states his love for bikes.

"Yes," I reply, wrapping my arm around Elizabeth's hip.

"I was the one who did your rear fender," Jackson says. I raise a brow at him, impressed. I had the drawings on my rear fender custom made. "I own my bike shop," he adds.

"Nice. Who knew Elizabeth here had a brother as clever as her." She rolls her eyes at me, then looks back to her family.

"Elizabeth? Why does he call you that? You said no one does," Rebecca chimes in.

"He refuses to call me Lissie." She smiles. "I don't want to be rude, as I love seeing you both, but we were in the middle of something. I would love to invite you in, but maybe you can come back tomorrow?"

"They can come in while you patch me up," I tell her and turn back to the kitchen.

"Patch him up?" Jackson asks and walks past Elizabeth. He's taller than her small frame, which isn't hard to beat. Rebecca is even slightly taller than her.

"Yep, got stabbed." I sit back down as Letti hands me a bandage and offers a hello to both of them.

"I took a bit of nursing in school. I can help. I mean, if you're okay with that?"

Rebecca offers, looking at her sister.

"I think he needs stitches," Elizabeth says, biting her bottom lip.

"I don't," I inform her. "It isn't deep enough."

"Can I look? I stitched a few people up, so I may be able to help." I lift my shirt as Rebecca examines the wound. "I reckon you could get away with a few butterfly stitches," she says, rummaging through the first aid kit.

Jackson leans in and says something to Elizabeth, and she smiles at him and grabs his arm. I watch her the entire time while Rebecca stitches me up.

The ease she now has, compared to six months ago, is extraordinary. The way she's blossomed is something to behold. Her confidence radiates in every smile and gesture, reflecting a newfound strength. Watching her transformation into this vibrant, self-assured person has been a journey. A damn good one!

"You're staring really hard at her," Rebecca says quietly. I glance down at her as she finishes up. "There you go, all patched up." She smiles. "I won't tell our dad about this either." I raise a brow at her.

"We have to go, but it was good to meet you all," Jackson says. I nod to him, and he does the same back. They hug Elizabeth before they leave, and then she turns to me.

"We're leaving," I announce.

Chapter 41

Lissie

"I hate goodbyes with you."

Milo hoists his bag, slightly grimacing as he clutches his side. His wound seems forgotten as he moves with determination, ignoring the pain etched in his features. It's like he doesn't have a care in the world.

"I shouldn't have come," he states, guilt lacing his tone. His shoulders slump as if the weight of regret is pressing down on him.

"They don't know who Lissie is or where she lives?" Mason asks Milo for the second time since he announced they were leaving.

"No, I made sure," Milo replies.

I bite my nails as I stand there, my nerves getting the better of me. Letti wraps me in a warm hug, whispering goodbye. Mason steps forward, his expression serious, instructing me to call if I notice anything suspicious. And then there's Milo, lingering at the edge of the group, his eyes searching mine as if he's trying to say something but can't quite put it into words.

"Bye, Lissie," Letti says, hugging me extra tight before she and Mason walk out.

"Are you okay?" I ask Milo.

He keeps his distance from me. "Yes."

I rub my hands together to stop myself from biting my nails, my anxiety building. "Will I see you again?" I ask, my voice trembling slightly as hope invades my words. My eyes search his face for any sign of reassurance, my heart aching for a positive answer.

"No. I won't visit again," he says bluntly, his words cutting the air. "But you know where I live." With that, he turns on his heel and walks out the door without a touch or backward glance. A small part of my heart chips away, leaving an aching voice in its place.

No goodbye.

No, *I'll check in on you.*

Does he blame himself?

I don't blame him.

I know who he is, and a small part of me knows the dangers that being around him could bring.

Yet I choose to see him anyway.

I stand there as he walks out, taking a piece of me with him.

And I'm left wondering, *What did he want to tell me?*

A few weeks later, with absolutely no contact from Milo, I received a message from the lawyer saying I needed to go back to finalize the divorce paperwork. Apparently, Cody is ready to sign.

Honestly, I thought that would never happen. I haven't heard from or seen him in months. Not that I was hoping for either of those things to happen.

"You shouldn't be here." I turn at the sound of that voice.

Milo stands there, dressed in his leather jacket, boots that could probably kick down a tree, and black jeans that make you want to tear them off to see what's underneath.

But I already know.

How did I not hear him approach?

"I'm here for business," I tell him, hugging myself and looking back to the house that I shared with Cody.

"He signed the papers," he states.

"Yep."

"Good. No other reason for you to come back, then." I flinch at his words, and he moves until he's standing next to me. I peer at him from the corner of my eye because it's too damn painful to look at him directly.

"You never want to see me again?"

"No. You can leave anytime. The sooner, the better." I don't outwardly react to his statement, but inside, a new slice appears in my heart, a sharp pain that lingers. The coldness of his words echo in my mind, each syllable deepening the wounds in my heart. My face remains stoic, but my cheek tightens as I struggle to keep my composure, the hurt threatening to consume me.

He doesn't say anything else before he turns and heads down the driveway. I see his bike parked on the side of the road. He sits on it, starts the engine, and puts his helmet on. Not once does he look back at me. I pick up a rock and run a little way down the driveway before I throw it at him. He was just about to take off, but he stops, flips the kickstand down with his boot, and then tears off his helmet to glare at me.

"Fuck you, you mother fucking asshole!" I reach down to pick up another rock, and just as I stand to throw it at him, he gets off his bike and stalks directly toward me, his helmet gripped tightly in his hand. When he reaches me, both my hands are fisted at my sides. I squeeze the rock, and his jaw tics before his lips thin, and he leans in closer.

"*Leave*, Pretty Lady." His words are dripping with warning. "This life isn't for you. Stay, and I'll drag you down with me." His words make my brain stop in its tracks, their gravity sinking in. Milo is probably one of the smartest people I know, and hearing him sends a chill down my spine. The intensity in his eyes is undeniable, and for a moment, I am frozen, caught between the urge to flee and the desire to stay despite the risks.

"Why would you drag me down?" I ask.

"You know why."

I shake my head. "Tell me why *you* would drag me down," I push.

"Because I would never let you go." He turns and goes back to his bike.

Drag me down?

Little does he know, all he would have to do is ask, and I would willingly drop at his damn feet. "I'm falling for you, you fucking asshole," I scream at his back.

"That would be a mistake," he says, sitting on his bike and securing his helmet.

"Loving you is a mistake?" I ask.

He looks away from me and starts the bike. "Loving me is toxic."

"I can't help it."

"Yes, you can" are his last words before he drives off.

* * *

After walking into Letti's apartment, I sit on the couch. Nothing much has changed, but you can tell a man lives here now. Mason's smell is everywhere. His shoes are at the door, and his things are scattered throughout every room.

"How long are you planning to stay? I would have made your bed, but I didn't know you were coming," Letti asks as she sits down next to me and rubs her eyes.

"I only intended to fly in to finalize the divorce, but then I saw Milo." I sigh.

"Yeah, he's been even quieter and more broody since we got back. He stays at the clubhouse and hardly goes home."

"He told me to go home and to not come back," I inform her.

"Well, he has no right to say that to you. This is your home as much as it is mine." I know she's trying to side with me, but his words remain lodged in my mind.

I wanted him to want me.

That's the issue.

I didn't expect him not to.

"Can I shower?" I ask, standing up. "Oh, and can I stay?"

"Of course you can. I'll get the bed ready. Take your time."

I pick up my bag and head to the bathroom. Dropping the bag on the bathroom floor, I strip off my clothes. Turning the water as hot as possible, I step under it. The water heats up and burns my skin, but I don't pull away.

Ever so slowly, anger starts to simmer within me. I've been angry at a man before—my husband, for sure. But Milo evokes a different type of anger, one I can't quite put into words. It's deeper and more complex, and I struggle to fully understand it or even describe it. This anger isn't just about hurt feelings. It's entangled with severe disappointment, frustration, and a sense of loss. Milo has touched something I didn't know existed, stirring emotions that leave me feeling raw, exposed, and open.

After quickly washing myself, I step out and dry off. I reach for whatever clean clothes I have before I pull the door open to find Letti there, holding some bedsheets.

"Can I borrow your car?" I ask.

"Of course."

"Thanks."

"Lissie," she calls out as I turn away. I stop and look back at her. "Please be safe." I don't answer, so she waves me off. "Bye."

I try to calm myself down on the drive to the clubhouse. It's getting late, and the sun has already set. When I pull into the driveway, I find Morris standing there waiting for me. He has a beer in his hand, and he shakes his head when I turn off the car. Letti must have warned him that I was coming because he didn't look surprised to see me.

"Lissie, really?" he asks as I shut the car door.

"Where is he?"

"I didn't tell him you were coming. He's had too

much to drink." I swing my head in his direction. Milo will drink, but he never has *too much*. Not since I've known him. "You can leave and walk away; he will never know you were here."

"But I am here," I say.

Striding past him, I don't stop when I reach the bar area. I look around until I spot Milo. He's sitting on a stool at the bar, a drink in one hand, the other hand running through his hair. He's alone.

He doesn't know I'm here yet, and I wonder how much he's actually had to drink. Mason spots me, and he taps Milo's shoulder, making him raise his head. And before I can move another inch, he swings around on his stool, and those fucking eyes meet mine.

It takes him a moment to register that I'm really standing here. Everyone has gone quiet. You can hear the fire crackling not too far from where we are while people breathe heavily, unsure of what to expect.

He stands and has to steady himself against the stool. I guess I have my answer—he's had way more to drink than expected.

Mason goes to touch his shoulder, but Milo shrugs him off, pushing him away as he makes his way over to me. I smell the whiskey on his breath first, but not long after, I smell the familiar sandalwood and the leather that rubs off on his skin. He has anger in his eyes as he stares at me. Pure hatred. It almost makes me step away. Almost.

"Pretty Lady."

"Do you drink like this often?"

"Fuck you," he seethes. Now, I do take a step back. He throws his head back, and an evil laugh escapes him. "You should be scared, Pretty Lady. I'm a bad, bad man—"

"Prez." Morris steps up and throws an arm around his shoulder as he looks at me. "You should leave, Lissie."

A part of me thinks I should, while the other wants to know why he hates me so much right now.

"I'm going to kill him," he says to me.

"Who?" I ask, taken aback, but then realize who he's talking about.

"Lissie, please go," Morris insists.

I step up to Milo and place my hands on either side of his face.

"You fell for a fucking loser. You love a man who doesn't deserve you," he says.

"It's not him I love," I spit back.

His eyes go wild, and he leans in. "And it's not

my fucking fault I'm falling for a fucking married woman whose husband I plan to kill."

"I'm going, but only because you're drunk and mean right now." I drop my hands and step back. "Find me when you're neither," I say, walking off.

He doesn't say another word.

Chapter 42

Milo

"Fuck."

I was one thing I never thought I would be to her—mean.

To everyone else, yes.

It fucking pained me to do it.

But I need her to hate me, so she leaves and never comes back.

This fucking place is exactly what I said it was—a shithole.

She is way too good for this town.

So if I have to be mean to get her to leave, I will fucking become a monster. I will channel every dark and ruthless part of me, sacrificing my own peace to ensure she stays away. If that's what it takes to protect her, I'll embrace the role, no matter the damn cost.

I tossed and turned all night, and when I finally woke up, I drove straight to Letti's and let myself in. And now I stand over Elizabeth as she sleeps.

"Milo?" she says groggily, knowing it's me. She sits up and rubs her eyes.

"You'll listen, and I will leave, then you *will* leave," I tell her.

"Stop presuming you know what I'll do," she shoots back.

I shake my head. "Trust me, you *will* leave." Scrubbing a hand down my face, I continue, "I kind of never knew how to take you... or want you," I confess. "To me, you were always *his wife...*" My words trail off. "I started to notice you more and more, and then you started reading to me." I grind my jaw. "You were always too good for him, for this place." Her eyes soften at my words. "When you left, I was glad," I tell her. "It meant that he lost you when he never deserved you in the first place. No one really deserves you, Pretty Lady. You are above us all. You see things and are hella smart. Too smart for this town, that's for sure. While some of us will be stuck here forever, you got out."

"I'm here now," she says.

"And I hate that you are," I say with a groan. "I have your husband. I've had him locked away for the last six months. Once you sign those papers, I will kill him."

Her eyes go wide with shock. "Milo..."

"I also have the recordings of your sister that he was going to send out."

"Milo, please let him out. Wherever you have him, please," she begs.

"Do you love him?" I ask.

"No, of course I don't. But I don't wish him dead either."

"He wishes you were dead," I tell her. The number of times I have tortured that fucking dick because of the things he says about her, and it makes no difference. He still wants her dead.

"That's fine. One of us can always be the bad guy." She gets out of bed and stands in front of me.

"Milo, let him out."

"No."

"Milo, please."

"Once the divorce is final," I tell her. "He would never have divorced you because he wants your money."

"I worked that one out myself, Milo. It's one of the reasons why I left." She nods and reaches for my hand. "Please, for me. Let him out."

"Maybe."

"Now, Milo. Please." I huff and reach for my cell. She moves forward and rests her hands on my chest, staring up at me.

"I don't hate you for it either."

"You may if you see him... he's lost a few fingers and toes." I give her a grim smile. Her body tenses as I press call. Morris answers straight away, and I tell him to let the scumbag go. He's confused, and rightly so, but he does as I say.

Her arms wrap around me, and she hugs me tight. "Thank you."

Chapter 43

—————

Lissie

"It feels like home."

"I need to shower," he says.

"Can I come with you?" I ask. "I mean, you wanted to talk, and I'll need a shower before I have to see the lawyer today."

"Clubhouse or my place?"

"Your house." Grabbing a bag, we leave Letti's and head to his place. We're quiet on the drive. I'm not sure what to say. He let Cody live for me. Which I'm sure he wouldn't have done for anybody else.

When we arrive, I smile as I look at the house. I love this place—it's somewhere I could live forever.

"Why haven't you been staying here?" I ask.

He kicks off his boots and tears off his shirt as he walks up the stairs. He doesn't answer me, so I put my bag down and follow him.

When I reach his room, the shower is already running, and I easily see him through the open bathroom door. Deciding I don't want us to fight, I take off my clothes, enter the bathroom, open the shower door, and step in behind him. He doesn't stop me when I place my arms around his waist and pull myself to him.

"I think I love you, Elizabeth," he whispers, still not facing me, his head against the wall. "And I fucking hate that I do."

I flinch at his words. "Milo."

He turns around, and before I can say another word, he pushes me backward, slamming my body against the wall and picking me up. He wastes no time positioning himself at my entrance, and I'm already eager and ready for him.

That's the thing—I think I always will be for him. I yearn for his touch like it's ingrained in me, and when I don't have it, I miss it. Want it.

As soon as he slides into me, I wrap my arms around his shoulders and let him take control. He moves me up and down, each thrust deeper than the last, claiming me. All of me. I don't tell him that he's going too fast, that I can't keep up my breathing—it's rushed and shallow from the onslaught of emotions running through me right now.

Milo Savage just told me he loves me.

And that he hates that he loves me.

Maybe I hate that he loves me too.

Or maybe not.

Love.

Hate.

Those emotions can go and suck a dick.

But not his dick because that is currently mine.

I bite into his shoulder as I come. It didn't take long for him to get me there. It never does with him. He knows exactly what he's doing and how to do it. Perfectly.

He stops, burying his head in my neck, breathing heavily. "Don't hate me," he says quietly.

I pull back and look at him. "I don't hate you, Milo."

He lifts me up and off his cock, and when he places me back on my feet, he's gentler, careful with each movement he takes. He turns away from me and steps under the spray. I hear him mutter something to himself before he turns to face me again. "You need to leave." He steps out of the shower.

"What? Why?"

"Because I just changed my mind, and I am about to hunt down your husband and kill him." He grabs a towel and wraps it around himself. "And you should leave this town *now*." He walks out and leaves me standing in his shower, stunned and speechless. The warmth of the shower contrasts sharply with the cold emptiness settling in my chest as I try to process everything.

What the hell just happened?

As I step out of the shower, I stand there in his bathroom, unsure what to do. After getting dressed, I leave the bathroom and find him already dressed and shoving his feet in his boots. He turns to face me as his cell starts ringing.

"I'll give you a ride." He stands as he answers his cell phone. After a moment, his eyes find mine, and something has changed in them. "I want you to stay real calm," he says in a soft voice, his hand gripping the cell.

I look at him, remaining calm, at least for now. "Do you think you being an asshole right now is going to make me lose it?" I ask with an eye roll.

"Elizabeth." He says my name with such seriousness and takes a step toward me.

"Promise me you will stay calm."

"What is wrong with you?"

"That was Mason," he says. "He just found Letti."

"Umm, okay, was she hiding?"

"He found her dead in her bed."

I hear him say my name, but it doesn't register.

Dead in her bed.

Like my mother was.

Maybe I'm dreaming.

I slap myself across the face, hoping it'll wake me up, but I'm still standing here, staring into the eyes of the man who saved me many times from being alone in that house when I was married, but who is now the one responsible for breaking my heart.

"Say something, Elizabeth. You're going pale."

I can't even fathom forming words right now. Thoughts are piling up in the back of my mind, but none are reaching my mouth. I take a tentative step back, and Milo reaches for me, but I put my hand out to stop him. His arm drops back to his side, listening to my unspoken instructions.

He's lying.

He doesn't want me here, so he's lying to get me to leave.

"Talk to me," he says.

But again, I say nothing.

I pick up my bag and head for the door. As soon

as I reach to turn the knob and pull the door open, he says my name again. It makes me stop, and my hands grip either edge of the doorframe for balance.

"You're lying in order to get me to leave," I accuse.

Milo grabs my bag and throws it in the car. "We have to go. I have to find him," he says.

"Find *him*?" I rasp.

His dark eyes meet mine, and he lays his hand on my arm.

I shove him away.

I don't want his hands on me.

"Cody. I have to find Cody."

I shake my head. "Cody? Why?"

For the first time, a profound sadness clouds his eyes. "Because he killed her."

"No. No, you just let him out. You said so yourself."

"That was an hour ago. From where we were keeping him to Letti's is a thirty-minute walk," he explains.

"She could still be alive," I breathe, hopeful, but Milo shakes his head.

"Mason had to be dragged out by Morris. Morris is a wreck—Letti was his sister. I have to go. I have to find him." He opens the car door, and like a robot, I get in. He drives to Letti's apartment and I sit in the car as he gets out.

"Stay in the car," he orders me before he closes the door.

What is going on? My head can't wrap around what is happening right now.

Surely, it's all fake.

Pushing the car door open, I stand on shaky legs and walk up the stairs to her apartment. I find Mason sitting outside her bedroom door, his head between his knees and his chest rising up and down with each breath. He doesn't even look my way as I push the door open wider.

I hear Milo's voice and Morris's grunted response before I see her.

Blood covers the bed, and her feet are hanging off the side. A loud scream rips through me, causing both men to swing their heads in my direction.

"It's *your* fucking fault," Morris shouts at me with hatred in his tone. I turn at the sound of a loud smack and find Morris sprawled on the floor.

"Get up," Milo growls at Morris before turning to me and softening his tone as he says, "I told you not to come in here." He reaches for me and lifts me bridal style, cradling my head against his chest to keep me from seeing.

But it's too late.

There is so much blood.

Her white sheets were coated with crimson.

And Morris is right—it is entirely my fault.

Milo carries me out as a police officer arrives. He nods to Milo, and they exchange words, but I don't hear them before I'm moved again. He puts me in the car, buckles me in, and takes me away. Neither of us says anything as we arrive at the clubhouse. When he parks, he hits the steering wheel hard as Axe walks out. Axe opens my door and looks across the car's roof to Milo as he gets out.

"Keep her here. Don't fucking let her leave," Milo orders.

Axe nods and helps me out. My eyes are so blurry that I just let him guide me as if I'm a robot. He takes me to the room where I have spent so much time reading to Milo and shuts the door behind him.

I fall to the floor, curl into a ball, and cry.

This is all my fault.

Chapter 44

Milo

"She is the prize."

I hate that bastard.

There is absolutely no other way to describe how I feel about Cody. He is a thieving asshole. The real reason I hate him, though, comes down to a woman with curly black hair and eyes that would haunt the devil.

He knew what a prize Lissie was. She wasn't like any of the other girls at the school we went to. She was clever. Fuck, was she clever. I would say it's one of my favorite things about her. And to say I was glad when she left him would be an understatement. No, I was fucking cheering.

I've never bothered hiding my resentment for *him*, and he knows it's because of her. Cody asked me several times to stay away, and I did. But that didn't mean I stopped trying to get her near me at every opportunity. That complete asshole never deserved her, and he was lucky to have her love.

But he never understood *just* how lucky he was.

Not until he lost it.

He's easy to find, not that I thought he wouldn't be. I knew he would run straight back to his mother's house. I wait a couple of houses down as Axe's baby sister walks up to the front door, dressed in church clothes, and knocks. His mother opens the door, and that's when I shift and sneak around the back. Luckily for me, she lives on a decent-sized lot, so there are no nosey neighbors. I find him sitting on the back porch, a cigarette in his hand, and he doesn't see me as I sneak up on him.

"Hey, asshole," I say and hit him on the back of the head hard enough to knock him out cold. The moment his body slumps, I grab him and lift him up. He's lost a lot of weight since we had him locked up.

I wanted to kill him immediately.

But for her, I didn't.

I realize my mistake now, and I won't be stupid enough to make the same mistake again.

Bambi, Axe's sister, is already back at the car and holding the door open for me. Throwing Cody into the back seat, I climb in beside him and toss her the keys. She takes off and goes straight to the back shed at the compound. It's a building that is designated for killing and torturing, designed for easy cleanup.

Bambi comes to a stop and climbs out.

"Go and swap with Axe," I tell her, and she nods. She's young, but like her brother, she's loyal. Our families all know each other.

Carrying the piece of shit back into the room he was once held in, I throw him to the floor. I pick up a butcher knife and take pleasure in waiting for him to wake.

When he comes around, he sits up, holding the back of his head, where I'm sure a large bump has formed. He looks around, and I watch as his body tenses when he realizes where he is.

He still has Letti's blood on him.

And that makes me even madder. My fists clench, and my jaw tightens, my anger intensifying. A fiery heat rises in my chest, making my pulse quicken. My face flushes with the force of my growing fury.

"You," he breaths out. "You let me go. Why am I here?"

I point the butcher knife at his shirt. "How did you get that blood on you? And if you lie, I'll cut off your hand..." I poise before finishing, "... to start with."

"I fell," he says, clearly lying.

I swing my arm down hard. The sound it makes when it connects is loud. His eyes bulge in disbelief as blood starts to pour from his wrist and pool around his severed hand.

Did this idiot really think a man like me would bluff?

"I warned you. And now you will fucking pay for what you did, you piece of shit." I swing again, and this time, I go straight for his neck. His blood splatters all over me as he falls backward, the life already drained from his eyes.

"Well, fuck," Axe says from behind me.

I drop the knife to the floor.

On my way out of the shed, I tell Axe, "Bury him where no one will ever find the asshole."

Chapter 45

Lissie

"A broken promise."

Milo pushes the door open and walks in—blood coats his face and arms. I have pushed myself up against the wall, unable to move. My eyes are puffy, and my head is sore from crying. And all I can think about is that it's my fault Letti is dead.

"I asked you to let him go," I croak as I look up at him.

Milo walks over to me and drops down into a crouch so we're eye to eye. "You did."

"I asked you not to kill my husband," I whisper.

"I broke that promise," he says, still not moving from in front of me. "He is dead, and I will not apologize for that, even though I know it will hurt you."

A new range of emotions rushes through me.

So much fucking hurt.

Pain.

I loved Cody once, but I loved Letti more.

Of that, I have no doubt.

It feels like my chest will cave in and crack open, and with it, the pain will pour out. But that doesn't happen.

"This will not break you, Elizabeth. Do you hear me? It will *not*." Milo stands, walks to his chest of drawers, and strips his clothes off. I curl myself into a ball. I remember her kind smile, and then I remember Cody's.

"Lissie." Soft hands touch me.

I open my eyes to find a face that I've only seen a few times. I don't even know her name.

"I'm Bambi, Axe's sister. Do you remember me?" I say nothing. "You've been in here all day, and you need to move. Milo was too afraid to touch you. But he had to go. Letti's mother..." She pauses. "Letti's mother needed him. He asked me to stay with you. I need you to move, Lissie." Bambi touches me again, her hands soft and gentle. She goes to help me up, and I let her.

Standing, she puts her arm around my waist. "Milo doesn't know what to do. He's not used to emotions, but you really did a number on that man. He's obsessed with you."

"How can you be near me?" I ask.

The door opens, and Mason stands there. Bambi's hands tighten around me as Mason's blood-shot eyes lock on mine.

"The funeral is tomorrow. You need to be there," he announces miserably. He pauses for a moment before continuing, "It's not your fault." I don't know how he can have compassion for me in a moment like this. Both of us are so broken. "She would be so fucking mad if I was angry at you, it is not your fault. You did not control his actions," he says, then turns and walks out.

"He's right, you know." I push her hand away and nod. "Your sister is at Milo's House... she isn't allowed here. But I am going to take you to her."

My sister?

"Savannah," I whisper, then I nod and follow her out.

She takes me straight to Milo's house, where Savannah is waiting out front, still dressed in her uniform.

When I get out of the car, she wraps her arms around me and holds me tight.

I remember the first time I saw Letti.

And I remember the last.

As if it were all one.

It blurs my vision as well as my memories. They hurt. Hurt so much that I feel my heart being torn from my body.

She was a woman who showed me kindness when no one else would.

I'm not really sure how to stop loving her or Milo.

Or if that's even possible.

Someone's hand slips into mine, and I have to pull away. I hear the intake of breath from whoever it is, and I should care. But I don't.

It's not in me to care right now.

People around me are talking, and I look down to see my heels digging deeper and deeper into the ground. It's wet, and by the looks of the sky, it's going to rain again soon.

Very soon.

Running my hands down my black dress, I suck

in my breath and try to hold it, wondering what they see right now when they look at me.

Black hair with tight curls I could never manage until I got older, mascara dripping down my face. Blinking through the tears that won't stop soaking my eyes, I look straight ahead.

Where Letti is.

The one person who could make me laugh, the one person who pulled me from the darkness when all I wanted to do was to allow it to swallow me whole.

I feel the stares, and I wonder if they're judging me, thinking I shouldn't be here because *it's my fault.*

"You can leave," I manage to say to Milo, who I know is standing next to me. He mumbles something under his breath, and I stand tall where I am unable to move, my heels still sinking further into the damp ground until it feels like I am wearing flats.

"No." I hear him say.

Lifting my hand, I swipe at my face. The rain has started falling again. And as I look to where Letti is, I wonder if she knows that I love her.

I do.

The dark brown casket begins lowering into the hole. And I fall to my knees as it does. My dress is covered in mud, and my new black heels have fallen off my feet. Probably still stuck deep in the ground where I stood.

I want to crawl to the casket with her.

Why?

Fucking why?

I hate this.

The only good person to ever be in my life and love me with all my flaws is being buried as I watch with disbelief.

The rain becomes heavier, and my hair sticks to my face. My clothes are clinging to my body.

I can't look anymore.

I can't.

"It's time to go, Elizabeth." Milo doesn't wait for me to answer. When I glance up, I notice it's just us here now because everyone else has gone. He lifts me and carries me to his car. "I want you to stay with me," he says as he starts the engine.

"People I love die. Do you really want that to happen to you?" I say as the rain splatters the windshield, the sky an unrelenting gray. The clouds hang heavy and low, mirroring my somber mood. Each drop of rain seems to carry the weight of sorrow, turning the world outside into a blurred, dreary canvas.

"I would gladly take any death if it meant I got to

have you." I gasp at that. And just as I turn to face him, my cell rings. Looking at it, I see my father's name.

"He called yesterday. I spoke to him," he says, surprising me. "He's waiting for you with your sister."

"You let them into your house? You hate people at your house," I say, surprised.

"Not if it involves you."

He ends the conversation as we pull up to the house. I see my father, dressed in a suit, and my sister standing next to him. When I get out of the car, my father walks up to me and pulls me into a hug. I accept it, but I feel my heart break again.

"I always have room for you. Come home," he says. I nod into his chest, and when I pull away, I see Savannah has my bag in her hand.

"I packed everything for you. Go heal. Remember, you have a family now that loves you," she says with a sad smile.

I glance around to see Milo walking into the house. The door shuts behind him, and my heart breaks a little at the sound of the lock snicking into position.

Chapter 46

Milo

"How can she not see how perfect she is."

I couldn't stand there and watch her leave—I can only take so much. And that I cannot take because I want to walk out there, throw her over my shoulder, bring her into the house, and tell her how perfect she is, that this too shall pass and get easier with time. Even though everything hurts now, the hurt will lessen, and she will find a way to cope with it.

"Milo." She unlocked the front door because she has access. I put my hand on the back of the couch and squeeze it. "I'm leaving," she says.

"I know." I don't turn around to face her.

"Why won't you look at me?" She sounds broken. "Is it because of h-him?" Her voice cracks.

"He is not the problem... my fucking emotions

are. And how I wish I met you sooner, made you love me before you loved him."

She wipes at her face. "I do love you, Milo," she says. "That scares me more than I want to admit." Sucking in a breath, she continues, "But I married him when I was deep in my emotions after my mother's death. I never dealt with those feelings, and he took hold of them and manipulated me. I want to love you. But I want to leave as well."

"Leave," I tell her. She wipes at her face again. "Leave, and don't ever come back, Elizabeth, because if you do—"

"Goodbye, Milo. Thank you for showing me that love doesn't have to be under duress." I look down and hear her heels click as she walks out.

And I'm pretty sure she takes a massive part of me with her.

Chapter 47

Lissie

"It's a new me."

If you had asked me a year ago if I thought I would be living back in this town, I would have laughed at you and told you how crazy that idea was and that I would never do something like that. Yet, here I am, in the very same house I tried so hard to escape from, feeling better than I ever did when I lived here before.

Cody was declared missing, and since my name was never taken off the deed, the house is also mine.

While I was living with my family, I paid contractors to strip the house down to its bones and breathe new life into it. Every wall, every corner was changed, leaving no trace of *him* behind. The memories that once lingered in the old rooms were swept away with the debris, replaced by the scent of new beginnings.

A soft knock sounds on the door, stirring me from my thoughts. I rise and make my way to the door, expecting my food delivery. But when I open it, I'm met with a familiar face—Milo. I don't invite him in. Instead, I stand there and lock my eyes on him. "If you plan to live here, I can't *not* see you. I gave you a week to cool off, and it's all you're getting," Milo says as he pushes past me.

I've been back a week and haven't seen him anywhere. I watch, my hand still on the doorknob, as he takes everything in. It's not much right now, but it is mine.

I open my mouth to speak, but nothing comes out. I knew I would have to see him at some point, but I didn't expect it to be this soon.

"Tell me how you killed him. I need to know before I eat. Otherwise, I'm afraid it will come back up," I demand, shutting the door and crossing my arms over my chest.

"Do you really want the details?" I nod. "How long until your food shows up?"

I glance at my watch and back to him. "Twenty minutes."

I know he doesn't want to discuss it with me, but

he walks into the room I turned into an office. His fingers run along the wood of my desk before he meets my gaze. "He had blood on his shirt, and I asked him how it got there." He cracks his neck as he speaks.

"Okay," I say, trying to keep my emotions in check.

"I slit his throat because he lied about it. About Letti. But first, I took off his hand." I gasp in surprise. "I would do it again, and I would do worse. I want you to know that."

"Do you have any remorse?"

He shrugs. "No. My first thought was that you would hate me."

"Why didn't you just tell me this?" No other words are spoken between us for a few moments, just silence hanging in the air.

His eyes trace every part of me. I've seen him do this before, right before he makes his move.

"You should leave," I tell him.

I need space to process.

He's clearly taken aback, his brows pinching, but he nods. "If that's what you want."

"I do," I say it more for myself.

He steps away from my desk and toward the door, where I'm still standing.

"Find me when you're ready. I'll be waiting," he states before he walks past me.

"What if I don't want to find you?" I try to infuse the question with a little confidence.

"I hope you never fall in love in this town because I'll probably kill him too," he states categorically as if it is one hundred percent a fact.

I follow him outside and stand there as he gets on his bike. "Do you know how toxic that sounds? No woman wants that." He smirks at me. "I don't want that," I yell, then shake my head at myself.

He tips his head to me in silent acknowledgment before turning and riding away. As he pulls out onto the street, I notice a car pulling up. A woman I don't recognize steps out and begins to approach me.

"Hey, I'm Stephanie. I did your house. Well, my company did, but it's good to put a face to the voice," she says, extending her hand, and I shake it. "I just wanted to come over and introduce myself and possibly invite you out?"

"Out?" I ask, a bit surprised.

"Yes, my company is putting on a function for clients." She smiles warmly.

As my food arrives, I step inside. "Come on in," I say.

We start talking as I unpack the food. She's young, and I get good vibes from her right away.

"So tell me about yourself," I say.

Stephanie's face lights up. "Well, I have a son who is almost four and ready for school. I had him while I was in high school, so I didn't get to go to college. But I love what I do. It's been a journey."

"That sounds challenging. But you've done an incredible job with my house," I reply.

"Thanks! I really appreciate you saying that. I am so grateful for the opportunity you gave me. It's been good for my business," she says, her eyes shining with gratitude.

I nod, feeling a genuine connection with her. "I am glad to hear that. You deserve all the accolades."

"I love what I do and always aim to make my clients happy."

"I can tell, and that means a lot," I reply, smiling.

As we continue talking, I realize how much I like her. She is not just good at her job. This woman really cares. And that's hard to find in a person.

"So what will you wear?" Stephanie asks.

"No idea," I answer, pushing the sofa over to the wall, not liking where it was placed. She sits down as I study it, unsure if I should move it again.

"He is also invited... the one on the bike?" My eyes find hers, and she gives me a smirk.

"How do you know about him?" I ask.

"Everyone knows Mr. Savage, and most women want him. But it seems he's wanted the same woman for a long time, or so the rumor goes." She plays with the ends of her hair as she talks, a clear indication she is treading lightly on the subject.

"Mr. Savage?" I haven't heard anyone call him that.

"Yep. Mr. Savage," she replies. "We were told we always had to respect him and be careful around him. He runs this town." She hums. "Though he doesn't really talk to many people." Her eyes find mine. "Does he talk to you?"

Heat flashes in my cheeks as I remember him reading to me, but I don't say anything.

"Oh, he for sure talks to you," she says, giving me a knowing look. "Okay, let's go out and go shopping. You need the perfect dress."

"I don't want to dress for *him*," I state.

"I'm sure he doesn't want you to dress for him either..." she pauses, and the smirk lights her eyes before she speaks again, "He probably wants you naked." She laughs. "Come on, the place looks great.

Tomorrow will be a hit. Let's go and find something to wear."

While I am out, I run into Morris and freeze on the spot. But as his eyes meet mine, guilt hits my stomach all over again. He stands next to a woman I recognize—she's the one who helped me escape Cody that night. She offers me a soft smile before she whispers something to Morris and then walks off. Morris stays where he is, and I hesitantly approach him. Morris is intimidating—there is absolutely no doubt about that—and he was so angry with me.

"Lissie."

"Morris." He just stands there and stares at me. "How are you?" I ask, and the words hurt. *How well can you be when you lose someone you love?* Especially a sibling.

"Been better." I nod and hug myself, looking down at the ground, the hurt and despair of that night hitting me in the chest. Hard. "I don't hate you, Lissie." His words bring my gaze back to his. "And I don't blame you." Something in my chest cracks, leaving a gaping wound open and bleeding. "It's not you who did it, and it wasn't you who told him to do it. You can't be blamed for his actions. I was mad and hurt, but I don't blame you," he says, and my hands drop to my sides as I feel a tear leave my eye. I swipe it away as quickly as it was there.

"I loved her, you know." *You know* comes out more like a whisper.

"I know. We all did," he replies. "I'll be seeing you, Lissie." He walks past me and taps my shoulder as he goes.

And somehow, I feel lighter after talking to him.

A bit more like myself.

Chapter 48

Milo

"It's always for her."

I can feel the eyes on me.

I'm used to it, to be honest.

I've dressed for the occasion, so all the looks I am receiving right now are warranted. It's a black tie event, and I'm dressed in a black suit, with a black button-up and black tie. Black on black. I didn't own a suit, but I went out and purchased one.

I got the heads up that she was attending; I was not going to attend. I get invited to all this type of shit; but I never go.

But she is coming.

So I will, too.

For *her*.

Morris stands next to me, dressed similarly, but he is wearing a white shirt.

I spot Lissie the minute I enter—it's hard not to recognize beauty when you see it. Especially hers.

People talk to Lissie and constantly touch her, giving her hugs and gripping her hands to say congratulations on her house. I want to stalk over and pull her body to mine and wrap my arms around her. Instead, I stay where I am.

"Are you planning to say hello?" Morris asks. "I saw her yesterday."

My gaze flicks to his.

"You know I don't really blame her for what happened to Letti. I do *actually* like her."

A small woman approaches us, holding out two drinks and offering them to us. "Hey, I'm Stephanie. I worked on Lissie's house."

"I'm—" She waves me off. "I already know who you are. Do you plan to gawk at her all night or go and say hello?"

Morris coughs, and I turn to see him covering his smile.

"She's talking," I reply, and she looks over her shoulder before she turns back to me.

"She looks beautiful in that dress, right? Look at that man in front of her, eyeing her. Kind of like what you're doing right now."

"I'll just be…" Morris mumbles before he walks off.

"Now, Mr. Savage, I suggest you go and talk to her." She turns and goes to the next person to mingle with them.

I grip the glass of champagne in my hand as I scan the room for Lissie. She moved, and her back is now to me as she talks to someone else. How different she is now from the quiet mouse to standing here mingling with people, and they all love her. Most know her or at least know of her. She is a hard one to miss in this town, even when she was married to that fuckhead. I stare as she flicks her hair over her shoulder before she turns around, and those eyes find me. She smiles. It's soft, but it's gone just as quickly as it came. Then, she turns back around to continue her conversation.

"Just tell her you love her," Morris says, coming back beside me.

"What?"

"You loved her before she even met her husband, Savage. Tell her you love her," he says, then walks off.

Elizabeth turns around and faces me, and my gaze follows her as she walks past a few guys who all check her out. I grip the glass tighter and remind myself not to kill anyone for looking at her.

She is beautiful.

Deadly so.

Her white heels click louder the closer she gets to me, and I notice I'm alone.

She stops in front of me, glances at the glass in my hand, and then meets my eyes.

"Do you intend to say hello?" she asks.

"Hello."

My favorite color has always been the color of her eyes. For a long time, I believed black to be my favorite color—simple, elegant, and powerful. But all that changed the moment I gazed into Elizabeth's eyes. Their depth and vibrancy caught me off guard and captured me completely. I couldn't look away and still can't. It is like her eyes hold the whole world and shimmer with emotions and untold stories. From the day I first glanced into those eyes, there is nothing that can match their beauty.

"You came. I didn't think I would see you at a function like this. I know this isn't your scene." She turns to leave, but I reach for her wrist. Everyone else has been touching her, so I should be able to do the same. Her gaze shoots to my hand on her wrist before it raises her eyes to mine.

I step a little closer, still holding her, and lean down to her ear. I take in her scent—clean, fresh, sweet—before I whisper, "You look beautiful. So much so that I'm hard from a simple look, and I haven't even touched you yet."

Lissie sucks in a breath, pulling at her wrist, and I let it go.

"Not that type of touch," I tell her, stepping back.

Her cheeks flush pink, and I lift the glass, putting it to my lips.

"I have to go and see what Stephanie has planned for the evening, to see if she needs any help," she manages to say.

"Tell men to stop touching you."

"No. I'm *not* yours. It's not *your* place to give that kind of order," she bites out, and that's when I realize her fire is back.

"But you are, and you know it. You just have to get over the fact that you're mad at me, Elizabeth."

"I'm always mad at you, and must you insist on calling me that? You know I prefer Lissie." I hide my laugh. Her anger toward me is one of my favorite things.

"You may prefer your friends to call you that, but we both know the truth..." He pauses for dramatic effect. "I'm not your fucking friend." Her brows raise, but she doesn't say anything back.

No. I am not her friend.

I am fucking way more than that.

"Maybe you should accompany me. If other men touching me bothers you so much," she challenges.

I set the glass down on the table behind me, then place my hand on the small of her back. "You lead the way."

She does, and my hand remains on her back as she mingles. A few people go in to hug her, but she makes no move to step away from my touch. Men hold back from touching her, which I'm thankful for, but I am sure it's recognition of who I am that stops them. And I would hate to kill someone just to have her angry at me again, though I would do it. I don't care!

"And who is this?" one lady asks.

"This is Milo. Milo, this is my mentor, Amanda, who helped me start a new business."

"I'm sure it was easy. Elizabeth is very clever," I say to the lady.

Lissie moves just a little until her body is touching mine. I take that invitation and wrap my arm around her waist, holding her to me.

"It was. My best student so far. You make sure

you treat her well. I'd have her back any day of the week," she says before moving on to another group.

The evening was pleasant, and I met a number of people who I hadn't seen before, but the time spent with Lissie was a bonus.

Most people have started to leave, and only family and friends are left mingling now. Lissie turns in my arms, her hands sliding up my chest.

"This was nice, you, here."

"It was only nice because I could touch you."

"I'm glad you came. I was sick of being touched by other people." She smirks.

"But my touch?" I squeeze her hip, and she locks her eyes on me.

"Is welcome."

"Arghhh. Hate to interrupt, but we're wondering where we can continue the party."

My men and Stephanie are the only ones left now.

"I have a babysitter tonight, so I plan to get fucked-up," Stephanie says, and Lissie laughs into my shoulder.

"Fucked-up?" I raise a brow.

"Yes. Momma needs some alcohol and a good time." She holds up one of the bottles of wine and looks at Lissie. "If that's not *too* unprofessional."

"I plan to take off these heels and then pass out, but you all go. Have fun." I squeeze her to me as she tries to pull away. "We can catch up tomorrow," she says, attempting again to pull away. I look at Morris. "Take everyone to the bar. Put it on my tab."

Stephanie cheers before they turn to leave.

I release my hold on Lissie, and she places one hand on my arm to steady herself before she lifts one foot and pulls off the heel. She does the same with the other, leaving both on the floor and her feet bare.

"Are you not going with them?" Lissie questions.

"Now, why would I do such a thing when what I want is standing in front of me?"

She gives me a small smile before she picks up her shoes and then collects her purse. "So... where we going?"

I glance at her dress and then raise my eyes back to her face. "As much as I want you on the back of my bike in that dress, I drove my car."

"So unlike you," she teases.

"Yes, it's my other lady," I tell her.

"Let me guess, your bike is the main lady."

"Nope. You are."

When we get outside, she scans the parking lot, and I assume she is looking for my car. But I have a few cars, and tonight, I drove an all-black 1967 Ford

Mustang. I've had her for a while, and over time, I've restored her to the beauty she is today. Nothing will replace my bike as number two, but my Mustang is a sure third.

"Milo." My name leaves Lissie on a breath as she walks to the car. I open the door for her, and she gazes up at me as she settles in the seat. "I'd love for you to fuck me on it."

"You don't have to say it twice," I tell her, shutting the door and walking around to the driver's side. I drive like fucking crazy back to my place. As soon as we get there, I get out, leaving the headlights on. I open her car door, and she takes my hand so I can help her out. Leading her to the front of the car, the hood still warm from the drive, I slide my hands down the front of her.

"Are you still mad at me?" I ask, leaning in but not letting my mouth touch her. She's eager for me to kiss her. I can tell by the way her chest rises to meet mine, but I hover, not closing the last bit of distance between us.

"Yes," she answers.

"Why?"

"You lied to me, kept something from me," she tells me honestly. "Why would you do that?"

"Because at first you couldn't handle the truth.

And then it came down to knowing you were better than being stuck in this town."

"Are you saying you aren't?" Her eyes narrow, and I lift her chin so our lips are close.

"Compared to you, no. I made you read to me to be around you, and I'd do anything to be around you."

She blows out a breath I didn't know she was holding. "Milo."

I let my hand leave her chin and drag down her body.

"I'm not mad at you anymore, though my heart still hurts." She pauses, and I lean in to kiss her, but she stops me by pulling back and placing a hand to my lips.

"She didn't die because of you. And he had to die. That asshole was scum, the way he—" I shake my head at the thought of him hurting her in any way.

"I know. I went to a bit of therapy after, and I should probably go back, but I see now it's not all my fault. My love isn't cursed." Her legs squeeze me as I stand between her thighs. "But you already knew this, didn't you?"

"Of course I did. Your heart just looked for love in all the fucking wrong places."

I kiss her. I have to. It's not a want. It's an urge I know I can't stop. I've loved her since the first time I saw her, and I will love her for as long as she'll let me.

Her arms circle around me, and I pull her close. She comes willingly, her white dress sliding on the car as I join our bodies together. Our lips smash against each other, and she lets me take what I need from her without any hesitation or fight.

She was made for me.

And despite this life I never chose, I'm grateful for it.

Because without it, I wouldn't have had her.

And Lissie is all I have ever wanted.

In this life and the next.

Chapter 49

Lissie

"Kiss me."

He pushes my dress up, and as he breaks our kiss, he's slow with his movements, soaking up every single minute of it. He knows I'm impatient when it comes to having his hands all over my body, so I think he takes his time, purposely going slow, which drives me mad.

But that's okay.

I'm starting to realize I like the way he drives me mad.

I tried not to want him, but that's a really hard thing to do when your heart is missing someone you didn't even know had worked their way in.

His mouth drags down my neck, over my dress, until he bites my nipple through the fabric. He finds my G-string and pulls it off without once removing his mouth from my breast. I'm wet—there is absolutely no denying that—as his hand skates around my thigh and touches me.

My back arches, and my hands—that are planted on the hood of the car—itch to touch him, but his thumb puts pressure on my clit, and he pushes a finger inside me, then another.

"See, Pretty Lady, you like everything I do to you. Your body tells me so."

My body loves every single touch from him.

No other man has known how to touch me the way Milo does. I don't know if it's because he has more experience or the fact that he can just read my body's response to everything he does to it. Either way, it makes me go crazy.

His fingers slide in and out, and he continues circling my clit, touching all the right places. His mouth moves to my other nipple, and he bites it through the material, not a care in the world that he could possibly be ruining a thousand-dollar dress. And to be honest, I couldn't care less either.

"M-Milo." I can barely say his name, but he doesn't stop as he hums in response to me as I fall back flat on the hood of the car.

"Are you tired?" he asks, removing his hands from my body. "We haven't finished playing yet."

I watch in fascination as he removes his tie. Milo pulls it off with one hand while he starts to unbutton his shirt with the other. When the tie is removed, he offers me his hand. I lift mine and place it in his palm, then he nods to my other hand, and I give him that one, too. He wraps his black tie around my wrists, binding them. When he's done, he steps back and drops his suit jacket before he removes his button-up.

I suck in a breath at seeing him this way again.

It's been too long.

He is so beautiful.

But before I know what he's going to do next, he pulls out a knife and starts to cut the dress from my body.

"That was an expensive dress," I grumble.

"I'll buy you ten more," he tells me. "So that I can cut them off as well." He smirks when he slides the knife between my breasts, and I hold my breath as he carefully slices until my now beautiful white dress is hanging on either side of me, half on from the sleeves but completely open down the middle, just as he likes it. He places the knife on the hood of the car so he can remove his trousers. "Pretty Lady," he says, pushing back between my legs. I can feel him, but he pulls me down, sliding my ass along the car until he's right at my entrance, just the tip inside me. "I want to marry you."

His words make my body tense, and he notices. I stop breathing. *Marry me.*

I never once thought about marriage after Cody.

To me, marriage is a death trap.

I once loved Cody and saw a life with him.

But how wrong I was about that.

I don't know an example of a healthy marriage that even makes me want to be married again.

And yet, here is this man, telling me he wants to marry me, knowing everything and still wanting me.

"When you're ready, be prepared for me to ask you. This is the only warning you will get." I let out a long exhale. "And don't be so scared. They say the *second time is the charm*, and trust me, we *will* fucking work. I will read to you every night, and in return, you will touch yourself." He winks, and I smile. "Imagine the dress I would cut off you on our wedding night," he finishes as he pushes all the way inside me.

"No way, I wouldn't let you."

"As if you could stop me from having what I want," he states. "Actually, let me rephrase that... you are probably the *only* person on this planet who could," he adds.

I go to lift my hands, but he shakes his head.

"Keep them there."

I do as he says, then he pulls out and steps back, taking me with him. My feet hit the ground, and he lifts me effortlessly, turning me around so now my tits are smashed into the hood. He grabs my tied-up hands and adjusts them above my head, then kicks my legs apart, my ass now on full display for him.

"What about a baby?" he asks.

"What the fuck, Milo?" I wriggle my hands against the knotted tie, but at the same moment, he slides inside me, and I groan.

"You don't want my babies?" he asks.

"Fucking hell." I moan as his hips move.

"Not even one?" he pushes. "Think about it while I fuck you."

I can't think about it.

I'm not even sure if that's something I want.

Why is he making me question everything with just the slide of his cock? It's really unfair for him to be doing this to me right now, but I don't hear myself complaining, either.

Maybe I do want these things with him.

I feel like life sent me down a path I didn't quite agree on, but I took it anyway and made the most of it, and somehow, I ended up here—lying on the hood of a car, my hands bound, with a man whom I've tried to not see for so many years. But that doesn't mean he hasn't seen me. Milo has been a constant in my life, and I have never had to ask for it. I don't think he would purposely ever hurt me, not in the way that Cody did.

And I know I'm falling for him.

Being without him, not seeing him, was torture. How was I supposed to know that once I had a taste, I'd always want to go back? And not just because of the way he makes me come. No, it's everything else and more.

Milo would be a great husband and father, and I have no doubt about that. And I get the feeling that it's only with me that he would be that type of person. With everyone else, he is cold and calculating, barely showing his emotions, yet with me, he gives almost everything.

He slaps my ass hard as he pushes in. He is never one to rush, always making sure I'm pleased before he takes his own pleasure. He fucks me until I see stars, then continues until he does too. Not once pausing his rhythm.

When he comes, he pulls out, then unties my wrists, careful as he does so. When he gently flips me to my back, I lie there naked, watching him with sleepy eyes.

"You don't like family," I remind him. "And yet you ask me for a child."

He chuckles. "With you, yes. Fuck, I'd even love to have a cat with you. And I hate fucking cats." He picks me up and carries me inside the house.

I giggle. "Who doesn't love cats? They're cute."

"Their piss stinks, and they scratch your eyes out," he complains.

"And babies cry and scream all the time. They also piss and shit, which you have to clean up."

"If it was our baby, I'd be down." He winks and sets me on the kitchen counter.

"You have the ring already, don't you?" I ask, staring at him.

He is ever so serious.

I can feel it.

"I do," he replies, smiling. "I found it when you first returned. When we went shopping."

"You bought a ring months ago?" I question, shocked. My mind races, trying to figure out the timeline and how I missed this. The thought of Milo planning this fills me with a mix of surprise and excitement.

"I just knew," he confidently says as he goes to the freezer and pulls out a tub of ice cream.

"Can I see it?"

"No. First, I gotta make you fall for me the same way I've fallen for you. It's only fair. You have time to catch up." He winks, handing me a spoon.

Little does he know, I've already fallen.

I just need him to catch me.

But I have no doubt he will.

"Elizabeth." He leans in and licks the ice cream from my bottom lip. "I fucking love you."

Also by T.L. Smith

Black (Black #1)

Red (Black #2)

White (Black #3)

Green (Black #4)

Kandiland

Pure Punishment (Standalone)

Antagonize Me (Standalone)

Degrade (Flawed #1)

Twisted (Flawed #2)

Distrust (Smirnov Bratva #1) FREE

Disbelief (Smirnov Bratva #2)

Defiance (Smirnov Bratva #3)

Dismissed (Smirnov Bratva #4)

Lovesick (Standalone)

Lotus (Standalone)

Savage Collision (A Savage Love Duet book 1)

Savage Reckoning (A Savage Love Duet book 2)

Buried in Lies

Distorted Love (Dark Intentions Duet 1)

Sinister Love (Dark Intentions Duet 2)

Cavalier (Crimson Elite #1)

Anguished (Crimson Elite #2)

Conceited (Crimson Elite #3)

Insolent (Crimson Elite #4)

Playette

Love Drunk

Hate Sober

Heartbreak Me (Duet #1)

Heartbreak You (Duet #2)

My Beautiful Poison

My Wicked Heart

My Cruel Lover

Chained Hands

Locked Hearts

Sinful Hands

Shackled Hearts

Reckless Hands

Arranged Hearts

Unlikely Queen

A Villain's Kiss

A Villain's Lies

Moments of Malevolence

Moments of Madness

Moments of Mayhem

Connect with T.L Smith by tlsmithauthor.com

T.L. Smith

USA Today Best Selling Author T.L. Smith loves to write her characters with flaws so beautiful and dark you can't turn away. Her books have been translated into several languages. If you don't catch up with her in her home state of Queensland, Australia you can usually find her travelling the world, either sitting on a beach in Bali or exploring Alcatraz in San Francisco or walking the streets of New York.

Connect with me tlsmithauthor.com